Starry Night Kisses

D.L. DARBY

starry night kisses

d.l. darby

Identifiers: Print - 979-8-9869973-9-1

This is a work of fiction. Names, places, and events are either products of the author's imagination or used fictitiously. Any resemblance to persons living or dead, organizations, or events is purely coincidence.

Edited by Virginia Carey

Cover created by WallFlower Designs

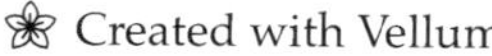

For the readers who are obsessed with their fictional book boyfriends but think they wouldn't like them in real life… Eric is ready to show you that anything is possible if you just believe.

content warning

This book contains light bondage, rope play, food play, talk of spousal cheating, and talk of infertility.

Please read responsibly.

a note from the author

This story picks up the night Peppermint Wishes left off. For the best reading experience, please read Peppermint Wishes first.

I wished upon a shooting star... and my whole world aligned when I found you.

— Unknown

Trying to explain how much I love you is like trying to count the stars.

— Unknown

evie

Snow begins to drift through the indigo night sky. Large downy flakes that sparkle and gleam as they catch the light from the fire pit in the backyard of my cousin Kendall's house. A shiver runs through me, though I'm not entirely sure it's from the cold.

Warm arms encircle my shoulders, drawing me back into a hard chest as I'm surrounded by the scent of wood chips and something slightly sweet but spicy that I can't put my finger on.

Eric Adams.

The man I kissed when the clock struck midnight. The man I just met less than a few hours ago.

Heat imbues my cheeks, spreading through my body as he leans down to murmur into my ear, "If it's too much, just say the word, and I'll back off."

Did I mention that before I kissed him, I may have rambled about how I'm not sure I'm ready for anything romantic right now? Despite my cousin's attempt to hook us up. Not only did I say *that*, but I also talked about how last Christmas, I thought *another man* was my soulmate.

I don't know how he could possibly be attracted to a woman rattling on about another man, but Eric told me he was patient—that he was content with just being friends for now. However, I wonder if my sudden New Year's kiss gave him the wrong impression.

I think it gave *me* the wrong impression.

Eric tastes like champagne and peppermint, and it's all too reminiscent of the Christmas I spent on Sutton Lake last year. He's not as burly as the grumpy man I encountered that magical weekend, but his dark brown hair and light eyes are similar.

I can't help but think of that mystical Christmas cabin every time Eric looks at me.

When I don't respond, he loosens his hold and steps back. Immediately, I miss his warmth, but remain silent as he settles at my side.

"So..." he trails off, and I glance over to see him staring into his glass while looking like he's trying to find his words. "Are you staying in town for a while?" he finally asks, shoving a hand in his pocket.

"I think so," I reply. "Honestly, I don't really know what I'm doing with my life now."

I went from a divorce to a man who left me when he got his secretary pregnant, to a wild goose chase trying to find a man I wasn't even sure existed before spending nearly the entire last year on an eat, pray, love journey overseas.

"What did you do before?" he asks.

I don't get the chance to reply as Eric's ex-wife and her husband Superman—er…Henry—approach us. Daphne is gorgeous, with bright blonde hair and blue eyes, and I don't miss the way they sparkle while she looks between her ex-husband and me.

"We're taking off. This little rosebud has been kicking all night, and it's way past our bedtime." She rubs her hand over her swollen belly, the size of it suggesting she's mere days away from giving birth.

Henry sticks his hand out to shake Eric's in farewell, then turns to offer me a warm smile. When I said Superman earlier, I wasn't lying. This man looks like Henry Cavill incarnate. I smile back and try not to melt as he says, "Nice meeting you, Evelyn."

Eric pulls Daphne into a tight hug, and I remember what he told me a few hours earlier about finding it hard to date because most women wouldn't understand his dynamic with his ex and her new beau.

Honestly, I find it really sweet. I've always been jealous of how close my cousin Kendall is with her friends. They're like their own little found family.

All of my *friends* abandoned me when my ex-husband decided to get his secretary pregnant.

Daphne hugs me next, whispering in my ear, "He's an amazing man. I think you'd be perfect together."

My face heats with her blessing as I watch them leave. My shared kiss with Eric earlier did not go unnoticed by the rest of the group, and I want to bury my head in my hands with embarrassment. I don't usually go around kissing random men, but it's New Year's Eve—well, day, now—and the champagne bubbles were fizzing in my stomach with the little peppermint butterflies that had settled there the moment Eric walked into my cousin's house earlier.

I have a lot of personal shit to work out. Do I want to try to add romance to the mix? I don't want to miss out on life, but it's just so sudden.

So was kissing him earlier, and you did it anyway.

Okay, fair. But I'm chalking that up to the heat of the moment.

Well, you probably did *give him the wrong impression. He said he was a patient man, didn't he? And then you kissed him* after *saying you weren't ready for anything romantic.*

"You're cute when you're arguing with yourself," Eric's amused voice cuts through my inner battle.

When I turn to look at him, he's chuckling as he watches me. "Please tell me I wasn't saying anything out loud."

"No, but it was pretty clear on your face. Plus, you were shaking your head and then nodding like you were weighing your pros and cons."

"Well, that's embarrassing," I deadpan.

"I found it adorable." His voice is soft, and he gently moves a strand of hair off my face. "I meant what I said earlier, you know. If you want to be friends, I'm okay with that. Because of the circumstances, we can call the kiss a heat of the moment thing," he echoes my earlier thoughts, and those damn minty butterflies break out their newly formed wings again. "We just met, so I get it. No need to make anything awkward…which I may have done earlier when I wrapped my arms around you. So, I apologize."

Eric holds my gaze solemnly, as though trying to drill in his words with the weight of his stare. Suddenly, I feel bad about being so weird after *I'm* the one who decided to kiss *him*. "No, there's nothing to apologize for. Like I said earlier, I've just gone through a lot in the last year. I'm sorry for being weird."

"Well, Evie, if you decide to stick around, I'd love to take you out for coffee and hear all about it…that is, if you want to talk about it."

Throwing caution to the wind, and knowing it's about to give us both whiplash, I smile and say coyly, "I thought we were going hiking?"

Eric mentioned doing the Oregon coast for Easter, but that's months away.

He lets out a loud laugh that sounds like warm marshmallow fluff to my ears. It's a weird thing to liken a laugh to, but the thought of food is never far from my mind, and it's literally the first thing I think of. "Sure, we can do that. I'll take you wherever you want to go."

evie

"What do you think, Bagel?" I fluff the large burgundy bow in the floral arrangement I made, the last of the finishing touches. I don't know Daphne or Henry or their style very well, but you can't go wrong with silk flowers and pampas. The neutral pinks, magentas, and beiges will be a perfect aesthetic addition to any nursery.

Once more, I ponder about whether Daphne even likes the color pink. However, she and Henry did just name their new baby girl Roselyn.

If she doesn't like pink, it's an easy fix.

Bagel lets out a woof of approval as I browse the silk flowers and artificial embellishments I've collected over the last two weeks. My kitchen table is messy with wrappings and ribbons, vases and fish bowls, and different colored decorative rocks and stones.

I've always liked decorating, and the travel blog

plus the social media account I started when I was abroad is at a standstill with adventures for now. So, I decided to pivot. I'm going to merge my travel accounts with staging and decorating ideas, and hopefully, some brands will want to work with me so I can keep my life schedule-free and come and go when I want to.

There's still money left from the sale of my parents' house, and for some reason, after the holidays, I decided to rent a condo in the city instead of looking into a travel van so Bagel and I could cross-country road trip and stay wherever we wanted for as long as we wanted.

At least it's just a month-to-month lease.

A buzzing sound comes from underneath a pile of ribbons. I hurriedly shove random silks and chiffons in a rainbow of colors out of the way until I find my phone and see Eric's name flashing across the screen. A photo of him and Archer stares up at me as I swipe my finger to answer the call.

"Hey!" I greet over-enthusiastically, wincing as the pitch of my voice resonates through my tiny kitchen.

"Hey there, I'm about to leave my house, and I was wondering if you'd like to go to Daphne and Henry's with me?" Eric's tone is hopeful, and there's a slight pinch in my chest before a flood of warmth encompasses my lungs.

"I would love that." Reaching up to rub my sternum, my knuckles graze the Northern Star pendant around my neck. I still haven't taken it off, thinking of Jonathan whenever I touch it or glimpse it in the mirror, but the more Eric and I talk, the less and less the other man enters my thoughts.

We hang up after he tells me how long it will take him to get to my apartment. Panicked, I run to my room to try and find a presentable outfit that isn't just the leggings and oversized sweater I've been living in for the past week.

It's been two weeks since we've seen each other—not for lack of trying. While my schedule is wide open, Eric's job is demanding, and he travels a lot. Honestly, it reminds me a lot of my ex-husband, Steven, and by the third time Eric had to cancel our plans, it left me with a lousy feeling—despite our long text conversations that have become our way of getting to know each other.

Emerging from my room dressed in black skinny jeans and an off-the-shoulder red sweater, I rush into the bathroom to brush my hair, using at least half a can of dry shampoo to eliminate my oily roots.

"Thank God I curled it yesterday," I mumble aloud, hairspraying a few random strands so they'll stop sticking straight out.

Behind me, Bagel wags his tail while watching me get ready, no doubt thinking that we're about to go for a walk.

"I'm sorry, buddy. We'll go as soon as I get back, I promise." I bend down and kiss him on the little peanut on the top of his head.

He gives me a woof of approval and turns to grab

a squeaky toy in the shape of a shark, shaking his head back and forth as he bites into it before padding over to his bed. It takes no less than three full circles before he plops onto the red and black flannel throw I laid down for him, and he props his head on the raised edge with the toy still in his mouth.

"Such a good boy," I coo. His tail wags in appreciation, and he closes his eyes, falling asleep in that manner only cats and dogs have the ability to do.

Returning to my kitchen table, I grab another beige pampas for the bouquet, fussing with it for another few minutes before deciding there are too many neutral tones and the colors aren't balanced.

Just as I put the finishing touches on my gift for Daphne, a text comes through from Eric.

Almost there.

After collecting my keys and purse, I shrug into my black shearling jacket before pulling on my knee-high black boots.

Did I have a sense of style pre-divorce? Yes.

Did that sense of style turn trash-panda chic afterward? Also, yes.

And after spending so much time in Europe, where I wore the same five outfits made of basics I could mix and match, I felt like *travel Evie's* sense of style was going to follow me forever. However, since arriving in Chicago and hanging around Kendall again, the urge to put myself together and dress a little cuter has hit me full force.

Sure, it has nothing to do with the fact that you're attracted to Eric and want him to think you're capable of dressing yourself without looking like a toddler who found clothes in the dark.

Eric is waiting by a white Chevy Silverado when I reach ground level. He's all smiles as he leans against his truck, looking positively edible in dark blue jeans and a tight black Henley beneath a charcoal peacoat. "Well, aren't you a sight for sore eyes?"

Shivers dance down my spine, and it's not because of the slight breeze in the air today. "Hi."

Well, that came out more timid than I meant it. Come on, Evie. You're not a shy girl. Get it together!

His perfect pearly whites gleam as his smile widens. "Hi."

He reaches for the bouquet in my hand, grabs the other to bring to his lips, and presses a soft kiss against the back of it. My cheeks grow warm. Eric's eyes never leave mine as he steps into me. "How are you, Evelyn?"

Oh, we're using my full name now? Excuse me while I melt into a puddle.

"I'm good." *There, my voice has returned with its usual confidence.* "How are you? Didn't you just get back today?"

"Yeah," he turns to open the passenger door and helps me in, "I have to leave again soon, too." He gives me an apologetic glance as he hands me the bouquet. "This is pretty. Did you make it?"

Ignoring the sting of disappointment at hearing that he's leaving again, I focus on my creation and smile with a shrug. "Yeah. I thought it would be nice for the nursery. I think I'm going to try and make a career out of it."

"Definitely planning on sticking around, then?" He grins up at me since I'm a little higher than him sitting in his truck. He's still in the open doorway of the passenger side, barely any space between us as he gives me his undivided attention. His light eyes sparkle, and I notice tiny flecks of green spotted throughout the blue of his irises.

"Was the renting of a condo not evidence enough?" I smirk at him impishly.

His eyebrows shoot into his hairline and he bites his bottom lip, something I've never seen a man do, but now all I can think of is what those teeth would feel like biting into my thighs.

"Don't be a smartass," he gently, but playfully, scolds as he buckles me in like a child. It's a considerate gesture, making me think Eric has a caring tendency, and I remember how he was with Daphne on New Year's Eve before her husband arrived.

The simple act sets my insides aflame and has me wishing that the giant bouquet wasn't in the way, because as he leans over my body, all I want to do is attack him with my lips.

Down girl! Geesh, you really need to get laid.

As if my pussy agrees, it clenches around air when I inhale Eric's woodchip scent. The air thickens between us as he pulls back, eyes dropping to my lips, which are parted slightly. His throat bobs as his gaze flickers back up.

A shrill blare like a nuclear warning snaps us both out of the moment, and he winces, shutting my door as he pulls his phone from his pocket. He answers it as he walks around the truck, pausing near the front to argue with whoever called.

I can barely make out what he's saying, but it sounds like it has to do with work. Dropping my eyes to the bouquet, I let out a sigh. My ex-husband, Steven, was always working long hours and traveling for his job. Maybe it wouldn't have been such a big deal if I had worked as well, but Steven hadn't wanted me to. He'd wanted me home all day, cleaning and having dinner ready for him on the table when he got home when he *was* in town.

It was a lonely life—for both of us, obviously, since he impregnated his secretary and moved her into our home before I even had my bags packed.

Is that something I want to go through again? Always waiting at home for my man to be available?

No, Evie. No, you do not.

"I'm so sorry about that," Eric says as he climbs into his truck. "Work is never-ending, unfortunately."

A noncommittal hum vibrates in my throat as I stare out the window, watching the busy streets as we head across the city toward South Loop, where Daphne and Henry's penthouse is. They have two homes—one here and one about thirty or so minutes away in the suburbs, not far from Kendall's home.

"Is everything okay?" he asks, pulling my attention across the truck.

"Yeah," I reply softly. "So, what *exactly* is it that you do for work, anyway?"

"I'm a lead cybersecurity specialist for a large corporation. They just moved their headquarters to New York, so I've had to go back and forth a lot. I think they're looking to merge with another big tech company there, which, unfortunately for me, means longer hours and a possible second home at this rate." He sounds frustrated—all his earlier playfulness depleted with one simple phone call.

"What do you do with Archer if you're always gone?"

Eric has the grace to look embarrassed as he admits, "I'm one of those assholes who got him licensed as an emotional support animal. I know I'm awful. But I can't bear to put him down in cargo, and I buy him his own seat. Honestly, I'm kinda like his emotional support human, so, really, it works out."

A soft laugh escapes me. Archer has separation anxiety, so it does track.

"But New York City is no place for a German shepherd. Not unless I want to buy a townhouse with a yard, and I don't like the city enough to drop that much money on a place."

I don't really know what to say to that. So, I just reply with, "Sounds exhausting."

He sighs, turning into a large complex and pulling the truck into guest parking. "It sure the hell is."

Eric helps me out of the truck, and it's not until we're in the elevator that I realize we're still holding hands. It feels natural, and the size of his palm against mine feels like our hands were made to fit together.

A woman who introduces herself as Maggie, Henry's mother, opens the door when we arrive. She and Eric exchange pleasantries before leading us further into the giant penthouse. I knew Daphne came from money, but this is a level of wealth that makes me feel out of place.

Everything is some shade of beige or cream. There are crystal chandeliers and matching furniture edged in what looks like real gold. Off to the right is a set of French doors leading out to a rooftop that looks like…

"Is that a garden?" I ask, shock lacing my voice. Bright, colorful flowers are in full bloom even though it's the middle of January, and beyond them, a turquoise pool is situated at the very end, overlooking the city.

Eric laughs. "Oh yeah, it's very popular. There are windows that keep the temperature where it needs to be, but they can be retracted in the summer."

What in the rich people?

"Evie! You made it!" Daphne exclaims as she comes out of a door on the other side of the living room, sounding well-rested for just giving birth a week ago.

When I turn, Henry is next to her with a bundle of pink in his arms, speaking softly to their newborn as he carries her over to show off his newest pride and joy. Proud papa doesn't even begin to categorize the look on his face.

Daphne looks like she just came from a photo shoot, dressed in a dusty blue maxi dress and a cream open-front shrug sweater. Her long blonde hair is piled on top of her head in a way I can only dream of doing with mine, and Eric's eyes warm when he sees her, sending a tiny flit of annoyance through me.

"Hi. Congratulations, by the way. She's beautiful." I return the hug she gives me before turning my attention to their little girl. "Hi there, little Roselyn."

"Is this for us? Oh my goodness, it's beautiful! I've never seen anything like this before. Did you make it?" Daphne asks, taking the bouquet from my hands. I'm glad I decided to stick with the beige and pink instead of making it too bright.

"Yeah, it's just a little something I played around with. I thought it would be cute in her nursery." I look over at Eric, who is cooing at Roselyn with a beaming smile. He moves like he's going to try to take her from Henry, but proud papa's arms tense, and Eric immediately backs off, holding his hands up in surrender.

"Oh, Henry!" Daphne swats at him. "Let him hold her." She turns back to me. "Do you wanna see the nursery? We have one here and at the other house; I'll have to commission you to make one for there, too. Maggie! Come look at what Evie made."

As we walk through the house, Maggie joins us, oohing and ahhing over the bouquet. "Oh, the ladies in my gardening club would just love this. We should hire you to come teach us how to make these!"

The nursery is swathed in cream with pink embellishments everywhere. It's filled with stuffed animals and toys that Roselyn is years away from enjoying, a fully stocked closet, and a crib that I somehow feel she won't need anytime soon. Henry seems pretty content with her nestled in his arms, and it wouldn't surprise me if he sleeps upright just so he can keep holding her.

I won't lie. It's hard being in this room. It takes everything I have to shove the tears down as I feel them pricking my eyes.

"Do you like to decorate? I can only imagine what your place looks like if you're able to make cool things like this. I can stage and pick out things, but I don't have a creative bone in my body." Daphne laughs as she places my gift on a shelf by the window.

Managing to swallow my grief, I nod, even though she can't see me. "I do. I love to create things and paint."

"Oh! Maybe you can paint something in here! I was thinking something like a fairytale woodland creature vibe, you know? Something mystical and magical," Daphne explains.

My first thought is how on earth I can manage to do it without breaking down, but after that comes the idea that it would be a great opportunity to showcase my abilities for my social media account.

You can't dwell on the past, Evie.

By the time we return to the living room, where the guys are now sitting on the couch, Henry—much to our surprise—is handing Roselyn over to Eric, fussing about him holding her head just right. Maggie is standing behind them, watching over Henry's shoulder and lightly scolding him about how Eric is an adult and can handle holding a baby.

Pain and something softer, warmer, battle in my chest as I watch Eric. His whole face lights up, and I swear tears shine in his eyes when he looks up at Daphne. "I'm so fucking happy for you, Daph."

His gaze slides to mine, rolling his eyes and shaking his head. With a smile, he says, "I know. I'm a sap. I just love babies."

Not wanting to lose my shit in front of a bunch of people I barely know, I awkwardly return his smile. "Yeah, a baby looks good on you."

"One day, it will happen. Don't give up hope," Daphne tells him as she sits on Henry's lap and wraps an arm around his neck.

I feel like I'm intruding on a special moment I'm not meant to be a part of. Something passes between Eric and Daphne as they smile at one another, and then to Henry, because he's obviously a part of their odd little equation.

Not many women are comfortable with how close we all are. I remember Eric's statement from New Years.

I want to be. The fact that they're still close doesn't bother me at all. But it's clear that one day, Eric wants a family, and I can't give that to him.

So, I might as well bow out before things get

complicated and sticky. I have a feeling I could fall for Eric just as easily as I did for Jonathan.

And I don't think I can handle having my heart broken like that again.

"Shit!" Eric curses as he hangs up his phone. "I'm so sorry, Evie."

"It's okay," I tell him, not tearing my eyes away from the window.

He'd talked me into having dinner with him once we left Daphne and Henry's, but his work called when we were on our way to the restaurant and told him he needed to go into the office.

It's probably better this way.

"No. It's really not. I feel like I keep fucking this up." I finally turn my head to see him white-knuckling the steering wheel. His elbow is propped against the window, and he sighs as he scrubs his face with his hand.

"Don't worry about it." I shrug when he looks over at me. "Friends. Remember?"

The rest of the ride is quiet, the only sound coming from the country music playing on the radio and the sound of horns as vehicles aggressively pass one another, fighting to get a fraction ahead of the other cars.

Eric insists on riding up the elevator with me when we reach my place, bending to play with Bagel as my energetic pup jumps on him and licks his face as soon as I open the door. "Oh, Archer is gonna be pissed at me when he smells you," he tells him with a laugh.

I attach the leash to his collar, and we walk Eric back down, waving at the concierge—a nice older gentleman named Phil—as we pass through the lobby, so that Bagel can do his business and I can say bye. I try not to put too much stock into the fact that Eric didn't just drop me off and leave, trying to spend as much time with me as possible, even though he needs to go to work.

"Do I at least get a hug?" he asks, opening his arms wide. He looks slightly concerned as I step into his embrace.

The earlier sexual tension between us has melted away—chased by the interruption to our plans, paired with the knowledge that Eric wants a family someday, and I can't give that to him…ever.

As if he can sense my hesitation, his arms loosen and he steps back, sliding his hands down to mine. "Is everything alright, Evie?"

"Yeah, I'm just more tired than I thought. Guess it's a good thing our plans had to change." I try to smile, but it's weary and doesn't reach my eyes.

If Eric notices, he doesn't push it and just squeezes my hands. "Okay, well. Talk later? I'm hoping I can stick around for at least a few days before having to fly back to New York."

The urge to kiss me flares in his eyes, bare and bright enough for me to see. But I rotate my hands out of his hold, pressing them against his chest as I lean up on my tiptoes and kiss his cheek. "Talk later."

Stepping back, I turn and gently pull on Bagel's leash so he follows me, pausing when Eric asks, "Did I do something? I can't help but feel like something's changed since we were at Daphne and Henry's."

"No," I say over my shoulder. "You haven't done anything wrong, Eric."

Once again, it's just me who can't get anything right.

evie

Draining the rest of my cab, I grab the bottle and pour the rest of the wine into my Olivia Pope-sized wineglass. Bagel sleeps peacefully in his bed in front of the fireplace media console, and there's a trashy reality TV show playing quietly as I sketch out ideas for Roselyn's nursery.

Over the past two weeks, Daphne has been adamant about getting me in there to paint. Eric says she's trying to make friends with me—which is silly because we're already friendly. She doesn't have to hire me to get me to like her.

My phone buzzes with an incoming text from Eric.

Once again, we haven't seen each other since he dropped me off. And although we've spent nearly every day texting back and forth, his absence is frustrating.

Even though I decided we can't take whatever it

is between us to a serious level, I feel a pull to him that I can't explain.

I absentmindedly play with my necklace as I read his message.

> If I have to go to one more dinner to schmooze the asses of men who have no idea what their own company does, I'm going to vomit.

A smile pulls at my lips as I sip my wine, setting my sketch pad on the coffee table and drawing my legs up to stretch out on the couch.

> Order the most expensive steak on the menu and get dessert to go. It's on the company dime, right? Better make it two desserts.

> You're positively diabolical. 😈

> How did you know I love dessert?

My heart skips a beat at the casual way he drops the L-word, even though we're talking about food. Crossing one leg over the other, my knee-high fuzzy socks soft against my bare legs, I think about snapping a photo and sending it to him.

Maybe it's the wine, or the fact that I'm wearing nothing but a pair of red, lacy, brief-style shorts with an oversized sweater—clothing that I feel sexy in. But I'm definitely feeling a type of way right now and feeling bold enough to do something about it.

Positioning my phone just right, I ensure the ambiance is perfectly set up in the frame of my screen. The soft glow of the fireplace, my white fuzzy socks, and my legs with the wineglass as the primary focus. Guys have a thing for bare thighs and knee-highs.

Before I can chicken out, I press send.

My dessert for tonight.

"No one said you can't have a little fun, Evie," I whisper to myself. "It's not like it means anything."

Eric's reply is immediate, and I nearly choke on my wine when I read his message.

I see something else in that photo I'd rather be having for dessert.

Our texts to each other over the past two weeks have bordered on flirtatious, but we've never taken it this far. Sure, we've exchanged photos, but it's usually of the dogs or of ourselves with the dogs.

My skin warms, that delicious dip of my stomach traveling between my legs, lighting up my lower body like a Christmas tree.

What else are you wearing?

"Fuck." The word slips from my lips as my nipples harden into pebbles, straining against the red lace bralette beneath my sweater as though trying to reach for Eric through the phone.

Are we really doing this?

> Unless that's being too forward? I apologize if so.

A sting of disappointment lessens my arousal just a little. Sometimes, I wish Eric would stop being so nice and just take command. I have a feeling if he did, we'd both enjoy the fuck out of it.

If it can't turn into something serious, though, do you really want to go down that road? Won't it make things messy?

The wine decides to answer my inner conscience.

You're adults. Stop tiptoeing around your feelings and just send him a damn sexy picture! Tomorrow's Evie can deal with the consequences.

"Consequences be damned," I mumble as I set my wine on the coffee table. Bagel picks his head up, his tail thumping against the edge of his bed, but I shake my head and tell him to stay as I head to my room, where there's a full-length mirror.

Peeling my sweater over my head, I simultaneously release the band holding my hair up, then position the mirror where I can easily pose in front of it. A thrill rushes through me. It's toasty and sets everything inside of me on fire as I sink to my knees. I fluff my hair and pinch my cheeks even though they're already flushed from the wine.

The lights that I have strung up over my bed

glitter in the mirror's reflection, adding an aesthetic appeal to the photo. My red undergarments stand out against the rich hardwood floor and my cream duvet.

It takes me a minute to get the perfect pose. Half leaned back on my shins, legs spread so my socks are visible, one hand thrust into my messy waves while I arch my back so my breasts strain against the bralette.

I've never taken a photo like this for anyone, and just the simple act of it makes me wet.

That's definitely something to explore.

I take a few shots, moving slightly for each one until I have the perfect one to send. Crossing my legs and leaning against the bed, I reach overhead for my sweater as I put the photo out into the interweb—knowing that Eric can ensure it never gets seen by anyone but him.

Setting my phone down, I only get the chance to turn my sweater right side out before Eric's reply buzzes through.

> Fuck, Evelyn. You look like a late Christmas present, complete with a bow and everything. I'm half tempted to come back for the night just so I can unwrap you.

Looking down, I realize that there is indeed a bow on my bralette.

> Goddamn, the things I want to do to you.

Like what?

I guess we are really doing this.

Abandoning my sweater, I push to my feet and climb on my bed, lying against my plush pillows as every nerve ending in my body comes alive with the thought of sexting Eric while he's out at dinner with his coworkers.

First, I'd untie that ribbon with my teeth.

My fingers trail down my body, reaching for the ends of the bows to see if they can even be unraveled. To my disappointment, they can't.

Then I'd kiss my way down your luscious body and bury myself between those legs, taking my time to show you how much I appreciate my present.

He's not even saying anything that borders crude, yet I can feel my wetness growing. I slip a hand beneath my underwear, my fingertips circling my entrance to gather the arousal before sliding up to start playing with my clit.

You still with me, baby?

Baby.

Fuck, why is that so hot?

Keep going.

Are you touching yourself?

My cheeks burn as I bite my bottom lip and snap a photo of my hand between my legs, then send it to him.

Fuck, Evelyn.

Do you enjoy knowing I'm rock hard at the table? Thinking of how wet you are and how badly I want to hear you scream my name when you come.

"Oh my god," I whisper breathily.

Yes, this is exactly what I need from him.

I need Eric to throw his nice guy tendencies out the window and command me to do things to myself while thinking it's him here doing them instead.

His texts start coming in one after the other, as if he can hear my inner prayers.

I can almost hear how wet you are for me, Evelyn.

Be a good girl and flip over. You'll need both hands for what I want to do to you.

Set your phone on your pillow. Get on your knees and use one hand to play with your clit while you finger yourself with the other.

A strangled moan leaves my lips, and I do what he says with no hesitation.

How many fingers did you put inside yourself, baby? One? Two? By the time I get back, you'll need to work up to at least three to fit me inside you.

"So cocky," I murmur, even though the image of his cock being that big rips a new flood of arousal from me, and I easily slip a third finger inside myself.

And before you go thinking I'm being cocky, this is what you have to look forward to.

A photo comes in, and it's clear that Eric went to the restaurant bathroom so we can have this conversation. In the photo, he's fisting the base of his dick. It's long and thick, the crown flushed and glistening with precum. My mouth waters at the thought of it sliding down my throat inch by inch until I'm gagging around him—and there's no doubt I'll choke on it. He definitely wasn't being cocky—just truthful.

The thought makes me thrust against my fingers harder and faster. I pinch my clit, rubbing it between my index finger and thumb as he keeps going.

I can't wait to fill you and feel that pussy strangle my cock. Fuck, I should have had you film yourself so I can see you getting off to the thought of that.

Are you almost there? I can just imagine you writhing beneath me as I lick my way between the valley of your breasts, sucking each of those perfect tits into my mouth as I fuck you slowly.

And yes, it will be slow.

Tortuous.

Agonizing.

Your pussy will be so well-acquainted with my tongue, my fingers, my cock, and whatever else I deem necessary to bring you to the edge over and over again before I finally make you see stars.

An unintelligible sound leaves my lips as I come around my fingers, pinching my clit so hard I can feel it pulsate with every convulsion.

As I come down from my high, I collapse into my pillows, picking up my phone with a ridiculously giddy smile.

I saw stars alright. 

Is that too casual for what he just did for me? Should I reciprocate now that my hands are free?

What part of me are you thinking about right now?

Feeling fearless, I tug my shorts down and prop my legs up, snapping a photo of my cum smeared on my inner thighs. From the way I'm positioned, Eric will be able to see the barest hint of where my mound dips and parts around my sex.

> Are you thinking about fucking me here?

Next, I yank down one side of my bralette until a rosy pink nipple pops out. I snap a photo of me palming my breast, pinching the swollen bud with the fingers that are covered with the evidence of my climax.

> Or how about here?

Moments later, Eric's name pops up as an incoming call, and shock spears my chest, gripping my esophagus in its icy fingers. A shred of doubt creeps in, but I swipe to answer and bring the phone to my ear.

"Evelyn Montgomery." His voice is low and husky as he grumbles my name. "You are fucking incredible. Do you know that?" I can tell that his breathing is heavy, like he's experiencing the same post-orgasm bliss that I am.

My mouth can't seem to form words, so I just breathe out a hum of content. I shiver with excitement, curling onto my side as he says, "If we keep this up, by the end of the week, I'm going to be begging you to keep me."

I already want to keep you.

The thought spirals an icicle of grief through my warm and fuzzy feelings, poking holes as it goes, deflating all my feel-good energy. Unbidden tears line my eyes, and I fight to keep Eric from hearing the sadness that suddenly takes over me. "You should get back to your dinner. Goodnight, Eric."

His reply sounds a little more earnest than just a second ago. "Goodnight, Evelyn."

evie

Swipe.

Swipe.

Swipe.

"He's decent looking," I mumble, shoving the last of my Snickers bar in my mouth. Tilting the phone toward Bagel, I ask, "What do you think?"

Bagel makes a low-pitched whine, slash woof, and shakes his head, sending his floppy ears flying through the air as they slap against his head.

"Well, they can't all be Eric, okay?" I hit like on the photo and exit out of the SparksFly app.

"Besides, it's just sex. That's all I want. No feelings. No strings. I just need to get laid."

Guilt creeps in as my phone pings, alerting me that the guy whose photo I just liked matched with me.

Things have been a little awkward with Eric after our night of sexting. He was supposed to have returned to Chicago by now, but got held up in New York for longer than he anticipated.

If anything, it just solidifies that his work is his first priority, as it should be, honestly. But at this point, he's told me he's coming back three times before turning around and saying he has to stay.

It's like Steven all over again.

Still, I feel bad. But if I'm being honest with myself, what I need right now is a distraction. I need to be touched and *filled* with no emotions involved.

And Eric is making me feel a whole lot of those lately.

The man is a bonafide golden retriever. Although, he also has the mouth and mind of a Doberman when he wants to exhibit a deeper, darker side that I feel he doesn't show others much.

I want him.

But he wants a family, and all I have to offer is myself.

My phone pings again, and Bagel lets out a low growl, jumping off the couch and grabbing a toy that he shakes back and forth before plopping down at my feet to gnaw on his squeaky shark.

"Geeze, buddy. Tell me how you really feel." I open the dating app on my phone to see that the guy who just matched with me has sent me a message.

Message Received

SUBJECT: DINNER?
HI, THERE.

FIRST OFF, I'D JUST LIKE TO SAY YOU'RE GORGEOUS. ACCORDING TO YOUR PROFILE, WE'RE LOOKING FOR THE EXACT SAME THING. SO WHAT DO YOU SAY?

DINNER TONIGHT?

I PROMISE I'M NOT A SERIAL KILLER.

LET ME KNOW WHAT YOU THINK.

-NATE

"See? This is exactly what I need."

And you need to make things clear with Eric.

I sigh. The sexting, no matter how good it was, has to be a one-time thing. I have to raise my walls. Have to tell Eric that we'd be better off as friends.

I can't give him what he needs, and he… Well… I'm not sure he can give me what I need, either. Because I won't be the clueless partner who sits at home while her significant other is traveling without her and–

Stop it, Evie. Eric wouldn't do something like that.

"Yeah, I thought that about Steven, too," I say out loud.

I've been doing that a lot lately, talking to myself.

I'm starting to lose it.

Quickly, I send Nate a reply.

SUBJECT: DINNER?

LET ME KNOW WHEN AND WHERE.

AND ALSO, I PROMISE I'M NOT A SERIAL KILLER, EITHER.

-EVIE

Bagel pauses in the destruction of his toy to look up at me, his big brown eyes filled with judgment.

"Don't look at me like that. It's a mental thing, okay? Be glad you don't have to worry about these types of things, sir."

All I get in return is another grumbled woof, followed by a symphony of squeaks.

So, what are you up to tonight?

The message comes through just as I'm finishing up my makeup. I nearly smear my lip gloss across my face when I see Eric's name pop up, as though he knows exactly what I'm up to, and he wants to remind me of his presence.

Hi there, remember me? The guy who made you come so hard you saw stars just by texting you?

I grab an old-school strawberry candy from the little dish on the coffee table, unwrapping it and tossing it in my mouth so I don't chew on my newly manicured thumbnail.

Should I tell him I'm going on a date?

Should I just rip the Band-Aid off now and say this isn't going to work?

Ever since that night, Eric has been all sweet sayings and proper gentlemanly topics of discussion. It's like the sexting didn't happen at all. Like he has a cinnamon-sweet Jekyll and a decadent, domineering

Hyde who only likes to show his face once in a blue moon.

My fingers fly over the screen before I overthink what I should say.

Nothing much.

Eric is almost eight hundred miles away. And we don't owe each other anything. For all I know, he could be hooking up with someone in New York.

I check my reflection in the mirror and smooth my dress. It's a simple black sheath with a square neckline and a slit that accentuates the curve of my hips. I've teased my hair to perfection, and as I slip into a pair of black pumps, I can't help but feel like a little hussy.

I've never gotten dolled up for a sex date before. As a matter of fact, it's been years since I've been this dressed up at all. Part of me feels exhilarated, while the other feels guilty.

Once Bagel is done doing his business outside, I give him a treat and check my phone once more.

Is it weird to say I miss you?

Fuck.

Something knocks on my ribs, trying to get to the organ nestled between my lungs.

Hope.

Longing.

A familiar sense of comfort that seems to be

present whenever Eric and I are within mere feet of each other.

As I stare down at my screen, thinking of a reply, a message comes through from Nate on the SparksFly app.

Message Received.

SUBJECT: SEE YOU SOON
I'M HEADED TO THE RESTAURANT. CAN'T WAIT TO MEET YOU.
X
-NATE

My heart does a backflip, and at the same time, my stomach goes cartwheeling in what seems like the other direction.

I'm a terrible person.

No, you're a human with needs, and Nate seems like as good a guy as any to fulfill those needs.

While the proverbial angel and devil on my shoulders argue, I reply to Nate, telling him I'm also on my way.

And I let the text from Eric remain unanswered.

"I honestly feel like I hit the jackpot. Seriously, you are a smoke show," Nate tells me for the fourth time since we sat down twenty minutes ago.

He's cute—with dark blond hair, hazel eyes, and

an aquiline nose with a small bump in the middle. But I find myself comparing his sandy strands to a chocolate bar, the green and brown specks to the bright, clear sky, and the slight downturned ridge to a straighter Grecian-like statue.

We're barely into our first glass of wine, and I already know I'm not going to be able to go through with it.

"Listen, Nate—"

"Are you ready to order?" our waiter interrupts us.

Nate already informed me that dinner was on him. *"None of that splitting the check bullshit,"* he'd said, which makes me wish I wanted to be here more than I do. He seems like an alright guy. At least someone who can roll me around in bed like I need—and perhaps stay on the *call for a good time* list.

So I order a steak and a baked sweet potato with a side salad. Nate also orders a steak, opting for steamed veggies and a regular potato. When the waiter leaves, he claps his hands together and waggles his eyebrows.

"I love a woman with an appetite," he says. It makes me laugh, and Jonathan instantly pokes back into my memories.

"What? I'm hungry."

"I do love feeding you."

The recollection has heat infusing my cheeks, and I rub my thighs together to alleviate the sudden need that settles in my core. Nate seems to pick up on my abrupt change in body language, and his eyes darken, dipping to where the lower half of my body disappears beneath the table's edge.

"I'm going to enjoy peeling that dress off you later," he says thickly, voice edged in a huskiness that wasn't there earlier.

As soon as my mouth opens to tell him I'm not sure that's where the night is going to lead us, a shadow falls over the table. Nate drags his eyes from me to look up, his eyebrows dipping in confusion before darting back to me. I follow his gaze, but hear an unmistakable rich tenor before I realize who's standing at our table.

"Evelyn?"

Eric?

Blinking rapidly, I stare dumbly up at the man looking at me as though he can't believe what he's seeing. His dark eyebrows are notched together, blue eyes glowing with confusion and betrayal. He looks fucking edible in dark jeans, a white button-up with the top few buttons undone, and a black herringbone casual sports jacket.

"Eric! Hi. What are you doing here? I thought you were in New York?" My chair makes a sharp squeak as I scoot it back and rise to my feet.

Way to go, Evie. You look guiltier than Bagel when he breaks into the treat container.

Eric swallows thickly, jaw clenching as he runs his eyes over me, then glances back at Nate, who's staring at us like he's about to get a show. When he turns his gaze back to me, his eyes have hardened in a way I recognize all too well.

He's putting walls up.

Remorse picks up a sledgehammer and slams it into my ribs, my breath getting caught in my throat with the force of the blow.

"I came back for a work dinner," he nods over his shoulder, "I was planning on surprising you later. But it looks like I'm the one who got the surprise."

"Eric–" I hate that I'm about to cry. I can feel the tears stinging their way up my sinuses, and my bottom lip begins to tremble.

"Don't worry about it, Evelyn." He smiles at me, but it's tight and doesn't show off his perfect teeth, then looks at Nate. "Sorry to interrupt your evening."

"Look, man…" Nate holds up his hands like he wants nothing to do with the situation unfolding before him.

"Seriously, it's not a big deal." Eric waves him off. "You two have a good night."

He turns away, and I take a step toward him, hand rising to stop him from leaving. But he strides away swiftly, returning to a large round table on the other side of the room full of people who look like they're discussing business.

Collapsing back in my seat, I plant my elbows on the edge of the table while Nate lets out a low whistle. "Soooo," he draws out the word. "Is that your boyfriend or something?"

Sighing, I shake my head. "No."

It's not a lie.

So then why do I feel like I got caught cheating?

eric

I like to think I'm a reasonable man.

I've given Evie her space. I've let her know what my intentions are. I've tried dropping subtle hints to urge her closer to the inevitable—to me…to *us*.

I like to think I'm a reasonable man.

However, at the moment, all I can think of is crossing the dining room to stab the fucking guy she's on a date with in the face with my steak knife.

'I'm going to enjoy peeling that dress off you later.'

I'm *going to enjoy hacking into your computer later to find anything I can to make your life hell, buddy.*

Seriously, what the hell is she thinking?

That fucking dress. Those fuck me heels. How her hair is styled in a way that will make any man looking at her think she looks freshly fucked.

She should be punished for entertaining the fucking fool.

It should be me sitting across from her right now.

Is she not interested in a relationship with me? Did I misinterpret the whole sexting thing?

I thought we had a great time.

Peeling my eyes away when dinner is brought to our table, I try to refocus my attention on work. Certain shareholders are nervous about the merger and the only reason I'm here is because, for some reason, these particular men believe me when I tell them the same thing my boss has been saying for months now.

It's the same reason he keeps sending me back to New York, too. *'You have the type of face that makes people feel at ease—feel that they can trust you,'* he'd said.

Well, right now the only person I care about getting to trust me is Evelyn.

I've never felt this way about anyone before—not even Daphne.

And I don't want to scare her away by being too intense, but I feel like I already *know* her.

Maybe it's because as soon as Kendall mentioned her cousin was traveling through Europe, I looked her up and followed her adventures. I got to know Evie long before she started getting to know me. I've read her blog, browsed all her photos on her social media—hell, I even went as far as to read the books she started recommending.

Creepy? Nooot exactly.

Stalkerish? Perhaps a little.

But by the time New Years rolled around, I was

already head over heels for the woman. It's why I told her I didn't mind being friends first, because I'd already concocted multiple versions of a plan in my head that ended with her and I in a relationship.

Then she kissed me…and it was perfect.

Until it wasn't.

Mere minutes later it was like she wanted to pretend it never happened. She's been hot and cold for weeks, so I thought giving her a little space was a good idea. Even though the only thing I've been wanting to do is hop the first flight home, barge into her place, and bury myself deep inside that perfect hourglass figure of hers.

After we sexted, it was *me* who backed off to see how she'd react. Unfortunately for me, she'd seemed perfectly fine with it. Like she just needed a release and I happened to message her at the right time.

Maybe that's really all she's after—a physical connection. I'm more than happy to give her that, and she *should* know that. So *why* is she out with another man?

Because perhaps she needs to be shown what she wants.

Or maybe you need to claim her how you want to and leave no doubt in her mind of your feelings.

My gaze strays to their table once more, and the smile on her face while the man across from her speaks animatedly is enough to turn my vision red.

I have to return to New York once dinner is over, but there's a little time before I need to be at the airport. A little time is all I need. Especially if I start texting her as soon as I leave the restaurant. I'll occupy the rest of her time so that she, hopefully, calls it a night and doesn't go home with that fucking dumbass.

I'm done waiting, Evelyn. Tonight, you're finally mine.

evie

The rest of dinner goes better than I expect it to. Nate chases away the awkwardness with stories of his YouTube channel, where he recounts true crime tales, and even asks if I want to get dessert to take home when it comes time to wrap things up.

He still pays for dinner, joking about giving me a bigger tip than the waiter, before telling me, "If you like the guy, just tell him. Because from the way he was watching you all night, it seems like he's pretty into you. I don't know if it's because you're not looking for anything serious, or what, but just remember, anything casual always has the potential to turn into lifelong."

"That's oddly…profound, Nate. Thank you," I tell him as he walks me to my car.

"Hey, I'm like an onion. I have layers." He pulls me into a hug like we've been friends for years.

"Take it easy, Evie. And if you end up not hooking up with him, give me a call." He winks before strolling away and getting into a Tesla a few rows down.

As soon as I turn out of the parking lot, a text comes through from Eric, and I have my phone read it through the car's speakers.

You know, you said you weren't ready, so I didn't want to push you. But if you wanted to date around, you could have just been honest and not strung me along.

Irrational anger ignites from the tips of my fingers down to my toes. Using speech to text I reply.

I'm not stringing you along! You're the one who's never here, Eric. You've been gone longer than you've been here in town. We've spent more time on the phone than in person.

Do I need to remind you that you're the one who kissed me on New Years? I told you I was a patient man, Evie, but excuse me if I won't wait on the sidelines while another guy 'will enjoy peeling your dress off later'.

My job is demanding, and I do apologize for that. But again, sometimes you seem like you want more, and other times you seem like you're content with being friends.

"Arrghhhh!" I scream into the air in frustration.

I'm well aware that arguing over text when it has to be read by a robotic woman's voice drains some of the seriousness from the tone of the fight. Still, I continue to parry his statements with jabs of my own.

Yeah, I took second place to a job once, I won't do it again. No, thank you.

And yes, I did kiss you, and then I panicked, okay? And yes, you've been a perfect gentleman, until the night where you insinuated you wanted to eat my pussy for dessert, commanded me to finger bang myself, and then pretended like it didn't happen.

But you're right. I'm the one who's being confusing.

Pulling into my complex's parking lot, I swing my car into its space with enough skid to make a drifter proud. I huff past the concierge, jamming my finger into the button for the elevator. My muscles strain with anger and pent-up sexual exasperation so thick it coats my skin like a layer of perspiration.

Is arguing with him really turning me on right now?

God, this is why I needed to get laid.

Bagel greets me at the door enthusiastically. I haven't even been gone for two hours, but I attach his collar and leash, intending to walk off the heady sensation crawling down my limbs.

I don't even get halfway to my room to change before there's a knock at my door. Bagel goes ballistic as I turn to answer it, thinking it's probably Phil, the concierge, with a package and I was in too pissy of a mood to realize he was trying to get my attention when I stormed through the lobby.

Yanking open the door, my heart stutters when I realize it's not the concierge at all.

It's Eric.

Blinking rapidly, I realize he had to have gotten in the other elevator before I even arrived on my floor. Which means…

Was he waiting for me?

Everything about him seems darker than usual—like the Mr. Hyde side of him is in full control as he storms in without an invitation, wrapping a hand around the back of my neck, while slamming the door with the other. I drop the leash as he crushes his soft lips to mine in a kiss that has my insides turning to lava. His hands are warm as they cradle the sides of my face, and he kisses me with fervent passion, as though he's trying to consume my soul for his very own.

I whimper against his lips, hands flying up to encircle his wrists. Bagel continues to bark at us, unsure if the man he's only met a few times means harm. When he finally pulls his lips from mine, I tell my pup to hush before returning my attention to him.

"Since you're obviously confused about my intentions. Are they clear now?" Eric speaks harshly against my lips, nipping at them as he demands an answer to his question.

With a gulp, I nod, sliding my hands up his arms to his shoulders. "Crystal."

Bending, he slides my skirt up to wrap his hands around my thighs, lifting me effortlessly before saying, "Good," against my lips.

Without breaking eye contact, he sets me on my kitchen table after swiping off most of the supplies I spent hours organizing. Tangling my hands in his hair, I can't even find it in me to be upset about it. I try to pull him back in for another kiss, but he resists.

His lips hover over mine, sparks of electricity creating delicious friction between them as he speaks. "I told you I'm a patient man, Evelyn. But if your plan is to go out there and see other guys, I might as well stake my claim now because the thought of another man with his hands on you drives me crazy."

The words are a purr and a growl all rolled into one as they vibrate against my lips. He slides his hands under my skirt, hooking his fingers into my simple black panties and peeling them off, pressing me down onto the table as he cups my hip and urges me to lift them. I'm so fucking turned on as he slides the material down my legs that I'll probably come the second he lays his sex-filled eyes on the most intimate part of me.

With a mind of their own, my hips undulate

against the air, searching for any sort of relief as my breaths leave my chest in labored pants. Eric bends over me, fingers trailing lightly up the underside of my arms as he gathers them together and pins my wrists to the table with one hand.

"Tell me to stop, and I will. However, if you don't, I'll take that as you want this just as badly as I do," he caresses the words against my lips.

An embarrassing mewl of desperation claws its way up my throat, and his mouth curves into a smile, brushing against mine ever so slightly. "Say it, Evelyn."

My legs cage against his hips, knees parting shamelessly to accommodate him as he wraps his free hand around the crease where my hip and thigh meet to pull me flush against the hard bulge in his pants.

"I want it!" I cry out, voice raspier than I've ever heard it before. I hook my heels against his backside, trying to draw him against me—to do anything to ease the ache between my legs as my pussy cries its own form of tears.

I'm bare and making a mess all over the new ribbons I got earlier this week. But I don't care as I thrash wantonly against the hard wooden surface. "Please, Eric. Please."

"That's it. I want to hear you beg for it." An odd feeling skates underneath my butt, and it takes me a second to realize that Eric is pulling a ribbon out from beneath me. He removes it methodically, pulling the silken fabric up against my pussy, tilting his hand inward as he watches it slide between my lips, coating them in my arousal.

My head tips back in pleasure, my eyes screwing shut as the ribbon brushes against my clit.

This is what I need.

The thought floods my brain in a warm wave.

I need a man to take complete control of me. Make me feel safe, while making me feel dirty at the same time.

"Please, Eric." He hasn't even touched me yet—not really—and I already feel like I'm seconds away from coming. "I need you. I need you to touch me."

"What else do you need, baby?" I feel him step away—hear him walk around the table, but I don't open my eyes.

Not until I feel the ribbon wrap around my wrists.

Eric ties me swiftly and expertly, looping the other end around the part where the top of the table meets the corner leg and securing it tightly enough that my upper body jerks sideways.

I'm spread over the table like his personal feast. He returns between my legs, eyes glued to my pussy that's pulsing, begging to be touched, licked, fucked, *anything.*

"Please, Eric," I beg, whimper, and whine all at once. "Touch me. Taste me. Take me. Whatever you want, I'm yours."

Baby blues snap to my face as his eyes widen slightly. "Say it again."

His hands feel rough as they slide up my thighs, parting my legs before he leans his elbows on the table on either side of my hips. My dress hitches all the way up to my waist, the tightness of the fabric getting caught on my breasts as he tries to push it higher.

"I'm yours," I pant, tugging at my restraints with the need to bury my fingers in his hair.

I can feel his hot breath at my entrance, his fingers curling into my ribs as we lock eyes just before he seals his lips over me. My head knocks back against the table, eyes screwing shut once more as my mouth falls open.

"Fuck," I whisper to the ceiling.

Eric starts slow, gently running his tongue through my slick center to part me, before flicking his way to the tight bundle of nerves swelling at the apex of my thighs. He uses the tip to swirl around my clit, gently dragging it back down to dip inside me.

His moan vibrates into me. "Fuck, baby, you taste so fucking sweet."

My toes curl as he maneuvers my legs over his shoulders before diving back in and yanking the top of my dress down, freeing my breasts. He pinches a nipple, rolling it between his fingers and tugging at the other while he licks and sucks me.

I flex my fingers, rotating my wrists to try to escape the ribbon because I want nothing more than to wrap my fingers in his hair and hold him to me while I ride his face. Eric seems to listen to every sound I make, abandoning teasing me in favor of going to town on my clit just how I like it.

"Just like that, don't fucking stop. Don't you dare

fucking stop," I moan, undulating my hips against his face.

And he doesn't.

Fuck me, he doesn't.

Not when he pulls the first orgasm from me. Or the second.

It's only after stars are exploding behind my eyes, my legs convulsing around his neck while I turn my face into my arm, biting down as I scream through my third climax, that he finally pulls back.

"I could keep this up all night. You're so fucking pretty when you're coming all over my mouth, Evelyn." Eric bends over me, kissing me lightly and letting me taste myself on his lips as he cradles my throat. "This will have to hold you over for now. As for your comment about coming second to a job, I put in for some time off starting next weekend. I have to go back to New York to wrap things up, but as soon as I get back, let's go on that hiking trip."

No, don't leave me again.

I want to say the words, but my brain is still foggy, and metaphorical stars are still sparkling at the edges of my vision. My eyebrows draw together in confusion as the post-orgasm bliss begins to wane.

Next weekend is Valentine's Day.

A dark chuckle rumbles from his chest. "Out there, there will be absolutely no mistaking how good I make you feel, Evelyn. In the woods, you can scream as loud as you want."

My pussy clenches, evidence of my multiple orgasms slipping from it and sliding in a wet trail down to my rear. Eric looks between my legs, his eyes darkening as he licks his lips like he's thinking about going back for fourths.

His thumb strokes a rough patch down my neck. "And if someone tries to come to your rescue," his gaze drifts to mine again, pure hunger etched into features, "they'll never be able to find us."

evie

Daphne collapses with a sigh onto the pink velvet chaise in the corner of Roselyn's nursery. "I swear, that child only wants her father to hold her. She gives a whole new meaning to the term *daddy's girl.*"

The corner of my lip twitches as I finish outlining a rose on the wall. The dusty chalk coats my fingers, a tiny bit falling on the warm maple floor as I return it to its case. I wipe my hands on the wet paper towel I brought into the room and clean up the mess on the floor before spinning around in my cross-legged position to face her.

"Daphne, can I ask you a personal question?" I keep my eyes focused on the floor between us, absentmindedly running my fingers over the cream shag rug I'd pushed back from the wall when I got started earlier.

"Mmhmm," she hums, eyes closed as she clutches a stuffed teddy bear. She looks seconds away from falling asleep, and I mull over whether to ask the question that's been on my mind since I saw Eric holding Roselyn. As I grapple inwardly with the decision, she peeks an eye open and smiles as she teases, "What's up, Evie? Do you wanna ask questions about Eric?"

I want to fall forward and sink my face into the soft, plush rug to hide my embarrassment. "Am I that easy to read?"

"Hey, I love this for you guys. As soon as Kendall mentioned you and Steven split, we both instantly thought you and Eric would be a good match. If you hadn't gone on your trip abroad, we would have set those wheels in motion a lot sooner." She winks and sits up, extending her arms and lacing her fingers together to stretch them behind her back.

Not gonna lie, it feels a little weird knowing that Eric's ex-wife had a hand in trying to set us up.

"Do you mind if I ask why you two didn't work out?" I avoid her gaze as I sheepishly look around the room. I can feel the flush of awkwardness creeping up my neck into my face, but Daphne tilts her head to catch my gaze, offering me a warm, understanding smile.

"We were together for a long time, but most of it was spent with me taking care of my mom when she was sick, and then grieving her death when we lost her," she explains. Her voice is melancholy, and her blue eyes go a little glassy as if she's thinking back to those harder times. "Eric was so good to me—so understanding—but I think we realized that maybe we pushed ourselves together because my mom really liked him. We honestly didn't have much in common. He worked a lot, and when he wasn't working, he wanted to be outdoors. I love to travel, but I would prefer to do it in style, if you know what I mean." She shrugs before laying back on the chaise. "That makes me sound vain, but there's no use in pretending to like a lifestyle that I just don't."

"It doesn't make you sound vain. If anything, at least you knew what you wanted and were honest enough to voice it."

Unlike my jerk of an ex-husband.

Shaking my head to clear all thoughts of Steven from it because the bastard doesn't deserve any more of my time, I think about last weekend and how Eric left me tied to my kitchen table.

Yes, *left me.*

Tied. To. The. Table.

I'd had to contort my body in ways I didn't know it could bend and twist for me to get free from my bindings.

My eyes flick up to Daphne to see her watching me with a vulpine grin, like she knows exactly what I'm thinking of. "He's a really good guy," she says. "He's kind and generous, and you'll never be left feeling unsatisfied. His tastes are a little particular—but I'm going to guess, judging by the look on your face right now, you've already found that out."

Her lips will split at the corners if her smile gets any wider, eyes sparkling with mischief as she cocks her head to the side. “Sorry, is it weird of me to speak of things like that?”

“Maybe a little…” I tell her honestly with a shrug. I don’t want to think of her and Eric together that way. Even though she’s remarried with a baby, I still can’t help the prick of jealousy that nudges my chest. “Can I ask why you guys never had any kids?”

The question is sour as it leaves my mouth, like the bitter bile you dry heave up when there’s nothing left in your stomach to purge during a bout of food poisoning or the flu.

Surprise takes over her pretty features, her mouth curving downward just a little as her brows notch together. “We tried…early on in our marriage.” She speaks slowly, as if she’s choosing her words carefully. Her gaze drops to her lap, where she starts to pick at her thumbnail—a trait we obviously share when we’re uncomfortable.

“You don’t have to–”

“No, it’s okay,” she cuts me off with a wave of her hand. “We wanted kids, but like I said earlier, my mom got sick, and things were stressful and hectic for a long time. Eventually, we just decided it wasn’t meant to be for us and stopped trying.” She looks back at me, mouth twitching as she asks, “Do you want kids?”

A swell of adrenaline floods my body with a harsh burn. It coats my esophagus, instantly clogging my sinuses and bringing an onslaught of hot tears that I begin to blink back. I open my mouth to respond, the words getting caught in my throat and resulting in a half-choked rasp instead.

Daphne frowns with concern, but says nothing as I attempt to get a grip on my feelings. Should I tell her the truth? Say that, yes, I want kids but can't have them. Do I tell her the whole story? Or just keep it to myself since I haven't even had that talk with Eric yet.

These days, as far as dating goes when you're our age, it seems like those are the types of things you talk about instantly—wanting kids or not. What if I tell Daphne, and then she tells Eric?

"You know, whatever you say is between us, Evie. I promise I won't say anything to Eric," Daphne cuts through my inner turmoil.

I release a breathy laugh, turning my eyes to the ceiling as I wipe under them at the tears that continue to gather. "Are you like a freaking psychic or something?"

She laughs and shrugs her shoulders. "When you've been in a group of friends like ours for a while, you begin to pick up on things without needing to be told."

The space between us fills with a heavy silence. It stretches for seconds, then maybe minutes, before I finally speak. "I can't have kids. Medically, I'm unable to."

I expect her face to twist in horror, for her hands to fly to her mouth, and a gasp to fall from her lips before she exclaims, *"Oh my gosh, I'm so sorry!"*

But Daphne does none of those things. Instead,

she holds my gaze and nods as she clasps her hands together and leans forward to rest her weight on her knees. "And how does that make you feel?" she asks like she's my personal therapist and I've just divulged a deep, dark secret.

I blink. "No…no one's ever asked me that… before."

A slight nod of her head has me continuing with the realization that all I've ever wanted was for someone to acknowledge that my feelings are valid. "It makes me feel… I don't know, like there's something wrong with me. Even though I know there's not—I know these things happen—but I still can't help but feel angry and resentful that I was created this way."

It feels good to let it out. Once upon a time, I wanted to go to therapy but couldn't afford it. And I've never had a group of friends to talk to about it since all the wives of Steven's friends just kept telling me to *keep trying,* like eventually, after multiple attempts and rounds of IVF, it would just magically happen, despite the doctors saying there was too small a chance.

I tell Daphne as much, and her eyes soften as she abandons the teddy bear on the chaise and kneels on the ground before me, pulling me into her arms without so much as a word.

Embracing her back, I let the tears fall. "I wanted to be a mom, *really* wanted it." My voice cracks, the words splitting between the hoarse rasps of my cries. "But Steven wouldn't even consider adoption. And the treatments made me so sick." I aggressively sniff, turning my head on her shoulder so I don't get snot in her hair. "A part of me was relieved when I found out about his secretary. *Relieved.* Isn't that stupid?"

"No, it's not stupid at all," Daphne soothes, rocking us back and forth as she strokes my hair like a child. "I'm so sorry all of that happened to you, Evie."

She's gonna tell Eric to run for the hills.

The thought has me pulling away, hastily wiping at my nose and eyes. She lets me go, sitting back on her shins as she appraises me.

"Is that why you pulled away from him after you saw him with Rose?" she asks.

My eyebrows flatten. "Geez, you two really *are* still close, aren't you?"

A melodic laugh fills the air. "I know. I know. It's weird. Most people don't understand it, but I can't imagine my life without him in it. And he really likes you, Evie. Really, *really* likes you. Talk to him about your concerns if that's what's holding you back." She nudges my knee. "Eric would be all for adoption."

"It's a little too early to have that talk, don't you think?" I mutter, turning to gather my art supplies.

My phone vibrates in the pocket of my sweater, and I pull it out while still sniffling to see that it's a text from Eric.

"I don't think it's too early at all," Daphne muses impishly as I read over the text.

Counting down until I have you all to myself for the weekend. Twenty-eight hours, fifty-seven minutes, and approximately five seconds by the time this text goes through, if you were wondering.

A pleasant calmness washes over me, filling me with a renewed sense of hope.

And, Evelyn?

"As a matter of fact, I'd venture to say that if you two just sit down and have a long conversation in person, he'll be putting a ring on it by the end of the year," Daphne states nonchalantly as she stands and turns to leave the room.

My head snaps up, catching her eye as she pauses with a hand on the doorframe and turns to throw me a wink over her shoulder.

I drop my startled gaze back to my phone as another text lights up the screen.

When I return, those dating apps better be gone from your phone.

evie

"So, where exactly are we going?" I'm unfamiliar with Illinois and don't recognize any significant landmarks as we head north. The snow has melted, and spring looks like it will settle in early this year. It's been warm for February, according to my cousin, and the only reason Eric has suggested we stay out in the woods for the weekend, I'm assuming.

"If I tell you, I'll have to kill you." Eric grins over at me, the vision interrupted by Archer shoving half his body through the opening between the front seats. The dog's body shakes with excitement as he leans down to lick Eric's face before moving to give me kisses, too. I feel bad that Bagel is stuck in the back, whining as he tries to reach me, but he can't because his little body is too short.

"Archer, get in the back, buddy," Eric gently reprimands him, pushing the giant shepherd back with his elbow. "I really need to get him one of those crash kennels. Worst dog parent ever, huh?"

I laugh. "I don't even know what you're talking about. Bagel is a passenger prince, so I guess that makes me a bad dog mom, too."

When Eric arrived at my door this morning with coffee, doughnuts, and a wicked smile that suggested he'd rather tie me up again than journey the few hours it would take to get to his *'magical campsite,'* I became all stuttered words and heart palpitations.

All that happened, however, was a sweet, chaste kiss in greeting before he helped himself to my kitchen to put the doughnuts on a plate and the coffee in mugs, even though we needed to get on the road.

Archer and Bagel played in the living room while we made small talk over breakfast. Yes, small talk. Even though what I really wanted to do, and I'm pretty sure he did too, was strip down and play a game of Twister in the bedroom.

Neighbors be damned.

The fact that he took two weeks off work in the middle of a huge shift for the company, just so we could spend time together, is probably the nicest thing anyone has ever done for me. As he looked over my sketch ideas for Roselyn's room and the photos of the progress I'd made so far, the fact that he seemed genuinely interested and continued complimenting my skills was just the icing on the cake.

Eric is kinda perfect.

Now, all I need to do is be a big girl and have the

'I can't have kids' discussion before this man makes me fall harder than I already have.

"I wasn't sure how you'd feel about sharing a tent, so I brought two, just in case," Eric says as casually as he would ask about the weather. "But I think we both know my preference on the matter."

"Okay, we have to talk about the elephant in the truck." I throw my arms up and slide my body sideways in my seat, hitching a leg up until it's forming a nine and I'm facing Eric full-on. I grab the bags of jerky I brought, giving a regular piece to Archer and sliding Bagel his own through the space between the seat and the door before tossing a piece of Korean-style pork in my mouth.

"You, sir, are like two totally different people in there." I point a long piece at him and twirl it in the air like a wand. Eric grabs my wrist mid-air and pulls my hand to his mouth, biting off a chunk of the tenderized meat while side-eyeing the road. The action makes me wet instantly. Eric hums in approval as if he knows it, rubbing his thumb lightly over my wrist before he lets me go.

"See? That! That *right there* is what I mean!" I cry once I find my words. "You are so laid-back one moment and then all dominant alpha male the next. Which one is the *real* you? Will the real Eric Adams *please* stand up?"

He lets out a long laugh. It's full and boisterous and makes his entire body shake with mirth. "This is the real me, Evie. Just your friendly neighborhood golden retriever in the streets and a dominant Doberman in the sheets, baby."

Baby.

In fear of melting, I shrug out of my jacket, letting it hang on my shoulders as I attempt to get rid of some of the heat radiating off my body. "Have you dated someone who's really into spicy romance books since Daphne or something?"

Did I just give away that I, myself, like spicy romance books—a hobby I picked up abroad?

Oh well. No shame in my game. Those books have unlocked kinks I never thought I'd be into.

Eric grins—he really has to stop doing that—like he knows exactly where my dirty mind has drifted off to. "I'm a cyber security specialist. I've seen some shit." He shrugs as we take an exit and turn left toward the woods. "I got curious."

Well, fuck. Now I'm curious, too.

"Does it bother you that we barely know each other and I'm overly familiar with you?" he asks suddenly, though the smile on his perfectly pouty lips denotes his playfulness hasn't left the building… err, truck.

I shake my head. "It's been six weeks. It's not like we haven't been talking and texting consistently, among other things," I mutter the last part under my breath, but he hears me anyway.

"How long did it take you to get untied, anyway?" He laughs, flinching as I reach over and smack his arm. Archer begins to bark, shoving his way onto the center console once more as his high-pitched yelps fill the truck. Bagel starts to bay. The loud shriek-like howl paired with Archer's pathetic cries has us covering our ears and sharing a look of sympathy.

"Too long," I shout over the noise, "and you're going to pay for that. And for making me get up so early today. I'm not a morning person, you know."

I swear he mutters, "I know." But I can barely make it out over the two ridiculous dogs who have created a two-hound band and are currently crafting their first chart topper.

How would he know?

I ponder the question as the forest grows thicker. The road is lined with fluffy Hemlock trees and other coniferous species, and the further we drive, the more I notice the naked, smooth, greige bark of maples peppered throughout.

I'm good at picking out certain things in nature, but if you asked me to write a detailed report on my findings in the forest at any given time, I'd get my paper back with a big, fat F circled in red.

Hiking is fun. Needing to learn everything about my surroundings while out on the trails is not.

There's a sign welcoming us to a national forest with a name I can't pronounce. Not long past that, there's a check-in station that Eric pulls up to with a smile.

"Hey there, Sampson," he greets, grabbing a yellow paper from his dash and handing it to the older gentleman.

Sampson smiles, the deep wrinkles in his face crinkling as his thick, bushy mustache wiggles. "Why hello, Eric." He leans down to peer through the open window and lifts his hand in a wave. "Hi there, miss."

"Hello," I offer politely.

Eric and Sampson fall into easy conversation, talking about how it's unnaturally warm this time of year and how the ground is dry, so we won't have to worry about snow. "But even so, it's still a bit early for campers to be in the area you're going to, so you don't need to worry about having any neighbors."

He gives Eric a wink before nodding to me. "Have a great time out there."

I don't know whether to be slightly disturbed by the older man's insinuation or if I'm looking too deep into the sparkle in his brown eyes. As soon as Eric's window is up and we're winding down the long road, I ask, "Come here a lot?"

"There's a lot of lakes and trails up in through here, and it's dog friendly. I keep Archer on his leash when we're hiking, his recall is shit, but I've never had a problem with any other dogs. It's like a whole different world up here, you know? One where I can escape the reality of work and the smell of the city. Just a man and his best friend, huh, buddy?" he coos to Archer, who has started to get restless in the backseat as though he recognizes where we're at and can't wait to stretch his legs.

"Why do you live in the suburbs, then, if you'd rather be in the woods?"

"Would you want to live in the middle of the

woods with no one around? Just your significant other and your dogs?" he answers my question with one of his own.

My reply is immediate. "No. I need human interaction. I wouldn't mind living somewhere with lots of land, so neighbors aren't right on top of us, but I definitely don't think I could be restrained to the forest with only you and the dogs for company... sorry." I look over at him as I laugh.

Eric's eyes have darkened and his knuckles are white where he's gripping the steering wheel. He's rubbing the lower half of his face while shooting me heavy glances, and the image causes my panties to grow wet.

"What?" My voice is breathy and I don't even know why.

"Do you even realize what you just said?" he asks, tone husky and low.

I replay my words, my cheeks heating as I realize that while he asked about a significant other in general, I responded as though we were a couple and mentioned living with him and Archer.

Just fucking own it, Evie. When did you become so scared to voice how you feel?

Against my will, my thoughts stray to Jonathan, and I think about how easily I spoke to the man I only knew for two and half days. My necklace is warm as I fish it from beneath my shirt and play with it absentmindedly.

Why am I so weird around Eric when I was never this way with Jonathan?

Maybe because Eric is here and single and wants to keep you forever.

"Evie?" My name on Eric's lips pulls my gaze his direction slowly. "Where'd you go in there?" He offers me a warm, yet slightly concerned, smile.

Shaking my head, I reach up and hook my arm around the underside of Archer's neck as he bumps his head against mine like he knows my thoughts skittered away to somewhere cold and sad. "Nowhere, I'm fine."

Eric seems to want to say more, but as we come around a corner, he slows his truck and pulls down a small dirt path just wide enough for the large vehicle. "You brought me out here to kill me, didn't you?" I deadpan, thinking about how I also playfully accused Jonathan of being a serial killer.

Without missing a beat, his voice is sinister and dripping with delicious promises as he replies, "Well, I did tell you that no one would be able to find us."

Somehow, that makes me shiver with anticipation instead of fear.

I'm about to respond when the trees thin and the scenery turns into something you'd see in a painting. There's a vast campsite with a rust-colored picnic table and a fire pit nestled on the sloped bank of a beautiful lake. The sun is high and bright, casting golden rays over the sporadic trees dotted throughout the grounds and highlighting the evergreens. The water appears more turquoise than blue beneath the yolky light, giving the lake a warm vibe, but I know the water is probably freezing.

"Wow," I breathe.

"Beautiful, isn't it?" Eric sounds proud, as if he's carved this little slice of heaven from the earth by himself.

Despite it being warm for February, there's still an early morning chill in the air that nips at my skin through my clothes when I exit the truck. "I hate early mornings, I hate the cold, and here I am, enduring both for a man I barely know," I mutter under my breath, pulling the hood of my flannel shacket over my curls.

Knowing we would be out here for two days with no shower, I opted for no makeup but at least curled my hair last night to make sure I didn't look like a complete trash panda. The last thing I need is a nursery of raccoons trying to adopt me as their own. I don't think Bagel would appreciate that much.

"Don't worry, I'll keep you warm," Eric speaks directly into my ear, sneaking up behind me like a freaking stealthy mountain lion. I jump and spin directly into his open arms. Without warning, he dips his head and presses his soft, pillowy lips against mine.

The kiss is immediately hot, and Eric takes complete control of my mouth, backing me against the side of the truck. Every cell in my body lights up and does a little dance, collectively groaning when he pulls away, lightly nipping the tip of my nose.

"How about now? Still cold?" He nuzzles my neck, grazing his teeth along the column as he peppers light kisses against my skin.

"Uh… Uh-uh," is all I manage, mind going completely stupid as he plays my body like a fiddle.

Every touch is strategic, from the way his fingers burrow inside my shacket to grip my sides over the thin, long-sleeved shirt I'm wearing to the way his other hand cradles the side of my neck he isn't attacking with his lips. His thumb strokes lazily over my pulse point, pressing ever so slightly when I moan.

"I can't wait to make you see stars later," he whispers against my skin. "Literally and figuratively."

Eric pulls back as the dogs rush back to our side, finished with their business and sniffing around the campsite to ensure it's all Archer and Bagel approved. "Let's get set up."

As much as I'd rather just climb into the backseat of his truck and have sex like we're teenagers, I oblige him and help unpack everything.

I'm a little confused as Eric keeps handing things down to me from the bed of the truck. Daphne mentioned wanting to travel in style, and while it's still tent camping, Eric has enough equipment to set up an entire household.

The two tents he brought are huge—like big enough for multiple families—and they connect via a tunnel that can be closed off from both sides. There's an outhouse with a full-on seat that goes over the sanitary container, and enough cooking equipment to fully stock a kitchen.

"Do you always travel like this?" I ask, looking

over the campground that now looks more like a woodsy-themed hotel room.

"No," he says as he sets up a cooking contraption over the fire pit. "Just pulling out all the stops for you, babe."

Excuse me while I melt into a puddle of goo.

He throws a charming smile over his shoulder, pearly whites on display, blue eyes sparkling with warmth as they drift down my body and back to my gaze. "Impressed?"

Arching an eyebrow, I shrug a shoulder and smirk before turning to head down to the water. "I guess we'll have to see how warm you can keep me."

Eric laughs and winks. "Oh, don't worry about that. I have gas heaters for both tents. It will be warm enough that you won't even need your pajamas."

I stop in my tracks, thinking about Bagel and Archer in a tent alone and how easily they could tip a heater over. "Gas heaters? Isn't that dangerous?"

Eric shakes his head. "No, it will be fine. There's a ventilation system and tip protection. Plus, a sensor in case there's not enough oxygen. Archer stays far away from it when we're out here by ourselves. Bagel will be toasty enough from across the tent, he won't even try to go near it. I promise."

I must still look worried, because Eric stands and walks over to me. "If it will make you feel better to have the dogs stay in our tent, we can do that." He leans down, rolling his forehead across mine and adding, "*After* we're finished consummating this relationship," as he passes.

"Oh, are we in a relationship now?" I ask in mock surprise.

"Yep." He pops his p. "I decided on the drive up. I'm done waiting. You're mine now," he states matter-of-factly.

Before I can reply, my stomach lets out a resounding grumble, reminding me that it's nearly time for second breakfast. Eric's laughter floats on the slight breeze as he turns. "How about some brunch? Then we can go for a hike. There's a place I wanna show you."

"Oh yeah? The place you're gonna murder me and hide my body?" I joke with a teasing, saccharine lilt.

"Nah, baby, the only thing that's gonna get murdered on this trip is your–"

"Whoo whoo whoo!" Both dogs break out in song, charging toward the water at a pair of geese floating around the bend. The fowl ruffle their feathers before taking off, and I call Bagel back before he tries to take a swim. He ignores me, continuing the ballad of his ancestor's hunting days. "Whoo whoo whoo!"

When I look back at Eric, who is moving our bathroom for the next two days closer to the water and away from our tent, he's wearing a wolfish grin that suggests he really does plan on murdering my–

"Whoooo whoooo whoooo!"

eric

"Favorite color?" I keep asking the questions even though I already know the answers.

It depends on the time of year.

"I don't really have a favorite. It kind of depends on the time of year, I guess," Evie responds, scrunching her nose as though she's just realizing this for the first time.

It's not that she's predictable. It's just that I've spent nearly a year studying her and already feel like I know her just as well as I know myself.

Creepy, I know.

I'm not a stalker, I swear. I just happened to find a woman who ticks every one of my boxes, and now she won't be able to get rid of me.

"Ooh, I have a good one!" she exclaims as she ducks beneath the low, naked branches of a maple right in the middle of the trail. Her tight jeans stretch across her voluptuous ass, and I try to quiet the groan that vibrates in my throat as I think about all the things I want to do to it later. "If you could travel anywhere in the world, where would you go?"

Well, that's easy. To the valley between your thighs where I'd become a permanent resident.

"Africa." Is the answer I give out loud. "Tanzania, to be exact. I want to hike Mt. Kilimanjaro."

A rabbit darts across our path, and Bagel lets out a long howl. It sets off Archer, and both dogs struggle against their leashes as they try to run after the poor animal. "Bagel!" Evie admonishes. "Leave the cute rabbit alone, bud."

She moves to the side as the trail widens again, looking at me as I resume my place beside her. "Kilimanjaro, huh? Are you wanting to do the Seven Summits?"

"Nah. I wouldn't mind doing Everest and Denali —maybe Vinson, too—but I'm not interested in the others. What about you? Same question." The sun shines through the trees, momentarily casting Evie in a glow that makes her appear angel-like.

She smiles over at me, and it takes my breath away.

Keep looking at me like that, baby, and our first time won't be nearly as romantic as I have planned.

"I just went everywhere I wanted to go. I haven't really thought about anywhere else. There was always the option of getting a travel van and exploring the States, but I'm not so sure about that now." She side-eyes me, the last few words of her sentence fading into a quiet lead.

"Would you rather be traveling in a van than be stationary here?"

This is one question I don't already know the answer to, and I find myself holding my breath in anticipation of her response. Scaling back on work is one thing; being completely inaccessible to my bosses and working remotely is another.

Job or woman. Job or woman.

While the answer is fucking simple, I can't provide for her and our family without a source of income, and while it's easy to get a job in my line of work, I've been with my company for too long to throw away that working relationship.

"I think I'm okay with being stationary for a while," she whispers, pulling me from my thoughts.

When I refocus on her, she's not looking at me but staring off the trail through the trees. "Is that water I hear?" she asks with a hint of a smile. "First one there wins," she says before taking off toward the rushing sound of the waterfall.

Archer begins to yip as we take off after her and Bagel, chasing them between the trees. Her peals of laughter join in with the dogs barking, causing the adrenaline in my veins to pump abnormally fast.

This right here is everything I've always wanted.

She's everything I've always dreamed about.

When I catch up to Evie, she's standing on the edge of a small hill that leads down to the water, taking in the scenery. The sunlight hits the spray from the falls, illuminating the space above the small pool at the base with a rainbow.

"It's beautiful," she says in awe.

"It sure is," I reply. But I'm not looking at it. I'm looking at her.

Cliche, I know.

But hey, I'm a sucker for a classic romance.

Evie looks at me from her peripheral, cheeks lighting up in a rosy pink hue as she turns her head to catch my gaze. I reach for her, intent on kissing her because I want to kiss her every minute of every hour of every day for the rest of our lives, but Archer and Bagel begin to chase each other—or try to anyway, getting their leashes tangled and nearly knocking us on our asses.

"Hold on, buddy," I tell Archer as I unhook his leash.

"I thought you said he has a bad recall?" Evie asks, releasing Bagel as well.

"If we were actively on the trails and he saw something he wanted to go after, like that rabbit, he'd take off and wouldn't return until he wanted to. But here, when we're just hanging out, he won't wander off," I explain.

"What if wildlife or another dog passed by here, though?" She walks down the hill carefully, sidestepping the large rocks that speckle the ground.

Fishing out a remote from my pocket, I hold up a hand in surrender and chuckle when her eyes grow wide in terror as she pauses mid-step. "It just vibrates, that's all. I'd never shock him. Henry's mother, Maggie, is the one who helped me train him."

Evie's eyes flatten, and she looks like she's about to argue that my logic doesn't make sense. However, as she resumes walking, her ankle gives out as she steps directly onto a rock protruding from the ground. Catapulting myself forward to catch her before she falls, we end up in a tangle of limbs, rolling the rest of the way down the hill.

A passerby would probably think it looks like something straight out of a romantic comedy.

When we reach the bottom, Evie somehow ends up directly on top of me, and I think it looks just like heaven.

Both dogs crowd us, whining with sympathetic yelps as they shove their noses at us to ensure we're okay.

"Sorry," Evie groans, clutching the front of my jacket.

Reaching up, I smooth her hair off her face. "You okay?"

"Yeah, are you?" She begins to lift herself off me, but I tighten my grip on her waist. "God, I'm sorry!" she says, and I tangle my fingers in her hair as I pull her down and roll us over.

"I'm not." I smash my mouth to hers, devouring her lips as she spreads her legs to make room for me between them.

Evie always tastes sweet—whether it's from the candy canes she kept sucking on during the New Years party or the strawberry candies she keeps in random bowls around her house. Every time I kiss her, she reminds me of sugary treats.

And I've discovered that I have one hell of a sweet tooth.

Evie

I can't get enough of Eric's mouth on mine.

When this man kisses me, I swear it's not for the purpose of rubbing our lips together because that's what you do in intimate situations. It's as though he's literally trying to consume my body and soul so that he can savor them, even when we aren't kissing.

Even though the sun began its descent a while ago, and we've started cooking dinner, all I can think of is *later*—when we finally get to go to bed and do other things.

If this man's kisses are this good, I can't imagine what it will be like when we finally have sex.

You're turning into a bonafide horndog, Evie.

"What's got you all dreamy-eyed over there?" Eric asks with a smirk as he prepares Archer's dinner—a mix of ground meat and vegetables and powdered vitamins that he makes himself every week.

"Nothing," I reply sheepishly, looking at Bagel happily chowing down his bowl of kibble. It's high-quality and expensive, but it makes me feel like perhaps I should start looking into preparing his food from scratch as well, even if he gets real food as snacks.

I return to chopping peppers for our stir-fry. I

wasn't expecting gourmet meals this weekend. Growing up, camping with my parents always consisted of hot dogs one night and the fish my dad would catch the next—anything to keep it simple and easy to clean up.

Eric, however, has an entire cooktop set up over the fire, complete with a large pot and a cast iron skillet because *'he really enjoys cooking.'*

Unwillingly, and I mean that word with every fiber of my being, my thoughts stray to Jonathan and how he fed me because being a caregiver was like second nature to him. I reach for my necklace, tipping my head back to gaze at the sky as the day bleeds into night and the stars begin to dot the heavens like specks of glitter.

"Is that necklace important to you?" Eric asks as he gives Archer his food before washing his hands at the station he brought. "You play with it a lot. Especially when you go wherever it is you go to in that beautiful head of yours."

"Do you believe in magic?" I ask as I hand over my cutting board of veggies.

Eric grabs a bowl from his portable refrigerator. I wasn't kidding when I said he brought enough gadgets to stock a kitchen. All we need is four walls and a roof, and we've got a house.

As he removes the plastic wrap from a bowl of marinated chicken, he cocks his head to the side. "Like magician magic?"

"No." I shake my head with a laugh. "Like… I don't know… Miracles? I guess?" I've told no one about my weekend at Sutton Lake or the things that happened afterward. No one knows about Jonathan and how we came together for one beautiful weekend, only for him to disappear from my life until I saw him a year later with the family he'd once told me had died in a car accident.

A skeptic would say he lied and played me for a fool.

But other things happened when I returned to that cabin, which suggested that although I might have been going crazy, no one was out to trick me. The entire town couldn't have been in on it.

"I think you're *my* miracle," Eric says sweetly, planting a soft kiss on my lips as he heads toward the fire pit.

"I'm being serious." I sit at the picnic table, leaning down to scratch behind Bagel's ears before he runs off to find his shark toy in the tent Eric set up for the dogs. It has a giant fluffy dog bed and numerous toys we both brought. Archer also heads into the tent, having finished inhaling his dinner, and grabs an elk antler to chew on before flopping down next to my pup.

"I am, too," he laughs. "Okay, but in all seriousness. I'm not really sure that I do believe in *magic*. I believe that things happen for a reason, but the world can be a pretty shit place. It's why I like to come out to the woods." He gestures around us. "Out here, it feels like none of the bad stuff can touch you."

"Have you experienced something you can't

explain, though? Like something that couldn't be possible *without* magic?" I press.

He's going to think you're a nutjob. Just drop it, Evie.

But I don't want to drop it. I want to tell Eric everything. *Before* we go any further.

What's the worst that can happen? He'll think I'm crazy and won't believe a word of it.

"I can't say that I have." He stirs the chicken in the skillet and peers up at me. "Have you?"

"You asked if my necklace was important to me. It is. But the story behind it is kind of… unbelievable. I've never told anyone about it." My eyes begin to sting, and a low whine turns my head to see Bagel staring at me from his place in the tent, like he always does when I think about Jonathan too hard.

"Well, I'm all ears. I'd love to hear about it. That is, if you'd like to tell me," Eric says gently.

"I think…that I'd really like to be able to tell someone finally." Bagel pads out of the tent and hops onto the bench beside me, nudging beneath my arms until he's snuggled in my lap.

With a deep breath, I begin my tale of the magical weekend I spent on Sutton Lake two Christmases ago. And I tell Eric all about the last man I'd fallen this hard for.

evie

Surprisingly, by the time the story is over, Eric isn't looking at me like he needs to take me back to the city and check me into a psych ward. He thoughtfully chews the last of his dinner, head tipped back to look at the canopy of stars that now covers us.

Finally, when he speaks, his voice is soft and kind as he asks, "So, this man, Jonathan, he just showed back up out of thin air with a wife and kid?"

"I know, it sounds like he played me for a fool, doesn't it? But I'm telling you, that isn't what happened." I stretch out on the blanket Eric laid on the bank for us earlier, having inhaled my dinner while telling my tale.

Eric shakes his head, setting his plate to the side and stretching out beside me. He folds his arms behind his head, the muscles of his biceps straining the fabric of his Henley. It makes me want to roll onto my side and run my fingers along them just to feel his sheer strength.

To feel safe in his arms.

"It would be easy to think that, but it doesn't explain the cabin or the people in town not remembering you," he muses, eyebrows dipping together in concentration like he's trying to figure out what could have happened.

"Exactly! Right?" I exclaim, sitting up and shifting toward him with my arms spread out. "And then a year later, there he is, looking younger and with the family he'd said he'd lost. I'm telling you, it was like a weird time portal or something. One that only worked when I arrived and then left. It, like, deactivated after that or something!"

Eric chuckles, reaching up to tuck my hair behind my ear. "And are you sad he didn't know who you were?"

The question feels heavy. Like Eric will base how he feels moving forward on my answer. His hand moves to cup my cheek as he shifts to his side, holding his weight on his forearm while running his thumb across my cheek. "Do you wish you'd never left? That you'd stayed and developed a relationship with him?"

My eyes fall to the swath of blanket between us, but Eric slides his hand beneath my chin to tip my head back up. "It's okay, Evelyn. You can be honest with me."

A shiver runs through my body as he calls me by my full name. It's almost like Eric's tell—how I know he's switched from that friendly golden retriever energy to the dominant alpha. Along with that, his voice grows deeper—huskier—when he speaks.

The sensual combination of it all makes me putty in his hands.

"I did," I tell him honestly, the words coming out in a whisper as his thumb slides up my chin to stroke along my lower lip. "I was angry at first, but it didn't last long at all. When I figured out what was happening, I could have remained silent—could have not told Tiffany to stay. Strategically placed myself in Jonathan's orbit to pick up the pieces. But that isn't the type of person I am. I was—*am*—happy that they're together and safe. He deserves that."

"And what do you deserve?" Eric asks, pushing to a sitting position. Our knees brush together as he scoots closer.

"I deserve to be happy, too." I don't even realize I'm crying until he brushes a stray tear away from the trail it's making down my cheek.

"Do you want to know what I think?" He grabs my hip and scoops under my knees, setting me between his legs and positioning my back to his chest. I rest my head on his shoulder and he rubs his cheek along mine, nuzzling my neck as he wraps his arms around me.

I don't just feel safe, I feel *seen* and cared for. It's such a small thing, but the intimacy of it means the world to me. "I'm glad it worked out the way it did because it led us to each other."

I tilt my head to the side to look at him from my peripheral. "You don't think we're moving too fast?"

"I don't think there needs to be a time limit on things like this. We are attracted to each other. We're compatible. Why do we need to go on ten dates before putting a label on it?" He rests his forehead on my temple and tightens his hold on me.

The fabric of his shirt is buttery soft as I stroke patterns up and down his arms. "I guess I'm just scared of falling so fast again. I think I'm guarded after everything that's happened. I don't want to get hurt again."

Sure, things are great right now, while we're far away from our adult responsibilities—or his, anyway. But what will happen when we get back and he returns to work? I don't want to be with someone who will always be absent.

"Evelyn, I've been waiting for a woman like you my whole life. If anyone is going to hurt anyone, it will be you hurting me." He pulls back again and kisses the spot where his forehead was resting.

A sharp sting pricks my chest, the hole filling with a thick, icy fog as I think about the conversation we need to have about kids. As much as I don't want to have the talk, this is the time to come clean about my infertility.

"Eric. About that..."

I feel him stiffen against me, his body going rigid even as I turn back around and lean against him, not able to bear seeing the disappointment on his face when I tell him the truth. "It's obviously way too soon to even be talking about kids, or having a family, but you should know before we take things further. I can't… I can't have kids."

The breath he blows out ruffles my hair as he drops his forehead against the crown of my head. "Baby–" he cuts himself off with a deep sigh. Moments pass where neither of us speaks, but Eric holds me to him, gently stroking his fingers back and forth across my arms.

Finally, he asks, "Do you want to have kids? Is being a mother something you're interested in?"

Guarded is the only word I can think of to describe the tone of his voice. My answer is a mere whisper, surrounded by a faint cloud of my breath as the temperature drops the longer the night stretches on. "I don't know."

Because, at this point, I don't. I've resigned myself to that life, giving up hope a long time ago that motherhood was something I'd ever be able to experience. I stopped dreaming of having a kid the moment my ex-husband cheated on me.

"Evelyn, I want you to know that isn't a dealbreaker for me." Eric nuzzles along the side of my face again, kissing my cheek as he squeezes me to him. "If you don't want kids, that's okay. And if you do, there's always adoption."

Relief pours through me, warm, happy, and adrenaline-laced to the point where a giddy shiver makes my limbs shake. "You'd be okay with that? With not having a baby directly from you?"

"Baby, I'm okay with whatever you're okay with.

If you don't want to go into detail about why you can't have kids, you don't have to, but just know that I'd never make you do something you don't want to do. And if you decide that being a mom is something you want, there are plenty of kids who need homes. Just because a baby doesn't come directly from us doesn't mean it won't still be our kid."

I'm aware that this conversation is hypothetical and a little ridiculous, given we've only known each other for six weeks, but I'm elated by Eric's answer and feel slightly silly that I made such a big deal about it.

As though Eric knows that, he guides my head to the side to look into my eyes. "I don't know what your ex-husband did to you to make you so scared to talk about it. But you need to know that you will never have anything to fear from me, okay? I want you to tell me *everything* that goes on in your mind. I want to know all your secrets and all your dreams. Because I'm going to make sure they all come true."

"You are literally perfect. You know that, right?" I laugh through the thin sheen of tears that line my eyes.

"Hey, I'm just following your lead. Except for when you clearly need me to take control of the situation. Like the night you tried to sleep with that Nate guy from the SparksFly app."

Alarms go off like giant red flags in my head, but my chest is surprisingly calm as I jolt forward and turn to look at him. "How do you know his name?

And how did you know we met on the SparksFly app?"

Eric shrugs and shakes his head, feigning innocence. "I don't know what you're talking about."

"Yes, you do, Eric Adams!" I playfully swat at his arm as he knocks me back to the blanket and covers my body with his.

"Nope. You must have misheard me." He kisses his way up my stomach over my thermal shirt, pausing between my breasts as he looks between them. "I'm about to become very acquainted with these," he sighs dreamily, the biggest smile stretching his lips. "Hello, new friends."

I laugh, the sound turning to a sharp gasp as he bends to nip at one through my clothes. But just when I open my mouth to encourage him to keep going, my stomach lets out a loud rumble.

Eric grins, gaze sliding to mine as he lifts his head. "Time for dessert?"

"I thought that's what we were just about to have?" I reply with a lilt and an arched brow.

His gaze darkens, roaming over my body before he pushes to his feet and offers me a hand. "I brought chocolate lava cakes. I'll indulge in more dessert later," he states, pointedly looking between my legs.

"Sex and chocolate. This is turning out to be a perfect camping trip." I don't release his hand once I'm on my feet, tucking myself into his side because I want to feel every hard inch of him against me.

Eric laughs. "Oh, baby, you have no idea."

evie

Eric wasn't lying about indulging in more dessert after our decadent chocolate cakes.

He tastes like dark promises of sinful delight as he backs me toward our tent, fingers tangled in my hair while he devours my lips. My skin warms like I'm standing too close to the flame in the fire pit, even though we're walking further away from the heat source.

"Are we really doing this in front of the dogs?" I joke when he pulls back to take a breath.

He chuckles. "No, we don't need to scar the kids."

I miss the warmth of his body immediately as he heads over to the other tent. Both Archer and Bagel are spread out in their bed, completely oblivious to the fuckery their parents are about to partake in.

Eric scratches both on the head. "Goodnight, you rascals. Archer, teach Bagel how to use the doggie door."

The scene floods my heart with a feeling I can

only describe as lo—no. It's too early to think of that word, and my brain is too muddled with the other L word—lust—to focus on anything else.

After he finishes saying goodnight to the dogs, Eric crosses the space swiftly, reaching to pull me back into his arms as he kisses me once more and directs me into our tent. "You have no idea how long I've waited for this," he murmurs.

A whine of frustration escapes my lips as he pulls away to zip the door shut. Eric's amused chuckles fill the heated space, sending intense flames to lick down my spine. "Patience, baby." He cradles my face tenderly, blue meeting blue. "I have all night to worship you."

"I want you now. I don't want to wait." My fingers fly to his jeans, scrambling to undo the button and yank the zipper down before lifting his shirt and roughly pulling it over his head.

If I could describe Eric in one word, it would be beautiful.

That probably sounds stupid, but every inch of him is hard, carved muscle and soft, unmarred skin that I want to run my tongue across. He's not built large like Jonathan, or slender like Steven, but a mix of the two that suggests he works out regularly but doesn't make his whole existence about the gym.

Eric lets me undress him, arms held out at his sides as he watches me lower his pants with a half-lidded gaze. "Fuck, Evelyn. Such a needy girl for my cock, aren't you?"

I peer up at him through my lashes, in that way

that drives guys crazy when you're on your knees before them, and nod. His thick, long erection strains between us, tenting his boxer briefs. I lick my lips as I reach for it, but Eric snatches my hand and pulls me to my feet.

"Sit on the edge of the bed and take your boots off, Evelyn," he commands before kneeling to untie his own and step out of his jeans, never breaking eye contact.

Once he's completely naked, cock pointed toward me like it's begging for me to wrap my lips around it, I reach for him again. He shakes his head, causing my lips to pull down in a pout. "But I want it."

He motions for me to lift my arms, and I do, letting him peel my layers off my body until my only top is a white lace bra. "I think you'll find that I'm a very giving man, Evelyn. And while I can't wait to have those pretty lips wrapped around my cock, I've been dying to eat your pussy again."

Eric sinks to his knees, putting his head at perfect level with my thighs. He brought us an actual bed on a frame, with an air mattress and a pillow top cushion dressed in soft cotton sheets. I grip the top of the fluffy down comforter, breasts heaving with each anticipated breath as his hands slide up my legs to undo the button of my jeans.

It's agonizing how slow he is as he removes my pants. Once they've slipped off my feet, I widen my legs to make room for him, knowing that the wet spot on my panties will be obvious when he looks.

And he doesn't just look. No. Eric worships the

sight, unmistakable reverence shining in his eyes as he slides two fingers against me to outline the spot. "Fuck, baby. Look how ready you are for me. Did the thought of my tongue on you make you this wet?"

With a groan, I lift my legs and hook them over his shoulders, relishing the hint of surprise that flashes across his face. "I've been in a permanent state of arousal for weeks now, buddy, and if you don't do something about it soon, I'm going to explode."

I feel his laughter as much as I hear it, hot and damp against my skin as he peels my underwear off before hooking his hands around my thighs, kissing his way toward that aching part of me that's been craving his mouth since the night he left me tied to my kitchen table.

Falling back to the bed as soon as his lips close over me, I can't stop the groan that leaves my lips as he gets to work, abandoning the foreplay in favor of the main attraction. He's a quick learner, even though I know he'd rather torture and tease me until I'm a writhing, moaning mess beneath him.

"Fuck, yeah. Just like that!" My voice echoes throughout the tent, piercing the thin material to climb into the starry night sky. The top of the tent has a zippered window covered in a thick enough material to keep the heat in, but it's clear enough that I literally *do* see stars as I come on Eric's tongue—just like he promised.

"How many do you think you can give me tonight, Evelyn?" he asks as he climbs up my body, his fingers replacing his tongue, swirling around my sensitive clit before plunging into me.

He swallows my unintelligible reply as he fills me, smoothing my hair off my face with one hand while the other lazily pumps into my pussy, winding the coil in my lower stomach once more before it even has the chance to come completely undone.

He leans back on his knees to watch the mess I'm making on his fingers, the unmistakable wet sounds of how turned on I am filling the air. "Tell me, baby. Were you this wet on the hike?"

"So fucking wet, Evelyn. Tell me, were you this wet on the hike? Did you walk through the forest with a mess between your legs?" My head thrashes against the bed as Jonathan's voice fills my brain. I don't want to think about him. I want to let go of the past and focus on my future, right here, with Eric.

I don't even register that he's stopped until his soft voice sounds above me, and his fingers grasp my chin to turn my head to him gently. "Open your eyes, Evelyn. Stay with me, baby."

The head of his cock lines up with my slick opening, pushing in slowly to part me as our gazes lock. "Stay with me, baby," he repeats.

There's something so sensual about fucking in the missionary position when your man knows how to roll and snap his hips just the right way and never breaks eye contact while he does it. Eric fills me until he's buried inside me to his root, stretching my walls around him with that delicious ache that sends tingles exploding through my body.

One of his arms drapes around the top of my head, and he strokes my hair softly with each gentle thrust. With his other hand, he pulls the cup of my bra down to free my right breast before lowering his mouth to the hardened peak.

Laying a chaste kiss there, he holds my gaze and says, "You feel even better than I imagined. I think your pussy was made for me, Evelyn *Adams*."

My walls clench around him at the sound of my first name with his last. Tangling my fingers in his hair as he dips back down to roll my nipple between his lips, I wrap the others beneath his arm and around his shoulder, using it as leverage to roll my hips against his.

He groans as the angle changes, and everything just…aligns. Eric slows even further, swapping his thrusts in favor of grinding against me as he releases my nipple and shifts a little higher.

I think it's the first time in my life I feel speechless.

"I told you I'd make sure you saw stars literally and figuratively." He grins as he whispers the words. "You're so fucking perfect. Taking me so well."

Every nerve ending in me climbs higher and higher, experiencing sensations I've never felt—red-hot sparks and electric pulses and the pure, erotic intimacy of staring into each other's eyes as we approach the edge together.

"Eric." His name comes out in a desperate, needy moan.

"I know, baby. I'm there, too."

"I'm going to–" My eyes roll to the back of my head as I come from what has to be the strongest orgasm I've ever received. My limbs shake as I cling to him, nails digging into his skin as my toes curl, while a tidal wave of pleasure pours through my body and over his.

Eric never slows or stops as he buries his face in my hair, quietly moaning as he empties himself inside me. The sounds he makes pulls another hot surge from me.

Fuck, if he sounds like this during such intimate sex, I wonder what he'll sound like once we get down and dirty.

We lay there, tangled together in a mess of sweaty limbs and heavy breaths. Eric manages to stay tucked inside me, careful not to lift his weight, just as I'm careful not to clench my walls and push him out.

Our intentions are clear. I may go back to the city with a UTI when the weekend is over, but Eric is going to stay inside me until he gets hard again, and we can go for another round.

"You're never going to be able to get rid of me after this, Evelyn," he whispers against my skin, trailing light kisses up my neck. "I'm obsessed, and I don't easily give up my obsessions."

"You already gave me your last name in the heat of the moment." I drag my nails up his back, delighting in the goosebumps that break out in their wake. "You have no intention of ever letting me go, whether I want it or not," I tease.

"Is that what you want?" He pulls back,

connecting our gazes as his cock jumps inside me. "For me to let you go?"

How is he hard again already?

"No, Eric. That isn't what I want." I smooth his hair off his damp forehead before pulling him down for a kiss. When we part, I mirror the devilish grin he's been flashing me since we met the best I can. "In fact, I dare you to keep me."

His hips roll against mine, causing my fingers to flex as my nails sink into his skin. "That, baby, is a challenge I gladly accept."

evie

Aromatic bacon and the sound of Bagel and Archer's playful yips rouse me from sleep. Eric's laughter as he talks to them drifts through the tent's thin walls, sending a shiver down my body despite how warm the heater kept the enclosed space through the night.

After multiple—and I do mean *multiple*—orgasms, Eric and I finally fell asleep what feels like not that long ago. However, the sun is shining high in the sky, signaling that it's probably late morning. I stretch, my sore limbs and aching muscles groaning in protest.

I haven't slept with anyone since Jonathan. It's just been me, my hand, and MGK—my vibrator. Don't judge. I was going through a phase when I named him, and afterward, it just felt disrespectful to call him anything different.

Eric worked my body harder than it's been exercised in a long time. That, paired with yesterday's walk, has my bones screaming in objection to the longer hike we're going on today.

Rubbing the sleep from my eyes, I sit up, knocking my forehead straight into something hanging mid-air. Eyes flying open in fear of it being a giant spider, I relax when I see it's a box of Sweet-hearts—the heart-shaped candies—hanging from a string.

That's right, it's Valentine's Day.

As the box spins, I see writing on it. Beneath the large bubbled *'Be Mine'* letters that cover the yellow heart on the front of the box, Eric has written,

...well, you already are, so I guess I got my gift early.

His script is more elegant than I'd have guessed for a man, while at the same time it's not surprising at all.

A stupid grin takes over my face as I push my chin into my shoulder, hiding behind both hands as I fall back against the pillows.

Girl, you got it bad.

Since Eric is cooking, I grab my bag and quickly wipe myself with a hygiene wipe. He may have pulled out all the stops to make this camping trip as glamorous as he could for me, but having no shower while having all this sex is something I'll have to get used to.

I dress quickly in jeans and a regular white shirt

with a black and red flannel before brushing through my curls and spraying the roots with some dry shampoo. Then I check my appearance in the hand-held mirror I brought. Something tells me it doesn't matter what I look like. Eric won't care as long as I'm looking at him with adoration and acceptance shining clear in my eyes.

Before I unzip the door, I realize I have morning breath and silently thank him for all the gadgets he brought while rushing over to the mini portable sink to brush my teeth before I go outside.

When I finally exit the tent, awe strikes me as I take in the transformation our campsite has gone through. There are lights in the shape of hearts strung from tree to tree, passing low over the tents and giving off a faint pink glow. The picnic table is decked out in a white tablecloth with pink and red hearts and bright pink disposable utensils. A bottle of champagne is chilling in a red bucket, with two glasses next to a carafe of orange juice.

Bagel bounds over to me with Archer in tow, both sporting bright red bows on their collars. "Good morning, my good boys," I coo, bending to give them head scratches and pets while they lick my face.

"Down, boys. The only one who gets to lick your mom is me," Eric jokes, turning from the fire pit to pull me into his arms and kiss the cheek the dogs didn't slobber on. "Good morning. Happy Valentine's Day."

Winding my arms around his neck, I press up on my tiptoes and kiss him, my body melting into his.

"Good morning. Happy Valentine's Day. Thank you for my candies. And for…all this." I gesture at the decorations. "You really went all out."

"I told you I was pulling out all the stops." He grins, returning to what looks like pancakes on the griddle.

"I don't know. You're setting the bar pretty high for our first official date, aren't you?" I arch an eyebrow and throw him a smirk over my shoulder as I head to the table to make a mimosa.

A bowl of strawberries cut into heart shapes sits next to the bucket of champagne, and I pluck a few for my glass before popping one in my mouth. "How long have you been up?"

He checks his watch. "A few hours now."

"You should have woken me up!"

"You're not a morning person, and besides, I kept you up all night. The least I could do is let you sleep in." He brings a platter over and sets it on the table, taking a sip from the glass I offer him.

My mouth waters at the sight of the thick, fluffy dough dotted with fat, juicy blueberries. It's not until I get one on my plate that I realize they are also heart-shaped. Picking up a piece of bacon from the second platter he sets down, I bite the end and wave the rest in a circle as I say, "Are you always this sugary?"

His brows draw together as he sits across from me. "You mean in terms of what I eat?"

I laugh. "No, and thank you for breakfast, by the way. This all looks amazing." I dip my knife into the butter dish and spread it over my pancake before reaching for the syrup. "I mean with all the decorations and themed stuff."

Eric continues to avoid my eyes as he dishes up his plate, calling the dogs over to give them each a piece of bacon. "Does it bother you?"

"Absolutely not!" I reach over the table to grab his hand, dipping my head to catch his gaze. "Eric, I love it. Thank you. Seriously. I just want this to be because you *want* to do it. Not because you're trying to impress me."

He rotates his hand to grasp mine, lifting it to press a warm kiss on the back. "I can promise you this is for no reason other than wanting to make you feel special."

"Okay," I relent.

"It's not too nice guy? I know you women don't like it when we're *too* nice," he jests.

I pop a piece of pancake in my mouth, my laugh turning into a moan as my head falls back while the tangy juice from the blueberries explodes on my taste buds, mixing with the sweetness of the syrup and the pillowy texture of the dough. "No, it's not too nice guy. Besides, I know there's a darker version hidden in there, too."

Eric chews slowly before washing his bite down with a large gulp of his mimosa. His voice deepens as he asks, "Is that what you'd like for your gift, Evelyn? The darker version of me?"

I don't know why, but I suddenly feel like I'm at the edge of a precipice. If I stay where I am, I know

I'll be safe. But if I jump off the edge… Who knows what the bottom will look like, even if the fall *is* exhilarating.

"Maybe." The word comes out in the barest of whispers. Quickly, I drop my eyes to my plate. "Is that what you'd like for *your* gift?"

When my eyes rise back to his, his smile is positively wolfish. "Baby, *you* are my gift."

Warm, gilded rays illuminate the trail as we hike up a small peak. The dogs happily romp ahead of us, their leashes continuously getting crossed, forcing Eric and I to switch places every few steps.

"You know, I was thinking about last night," Eric starts, a wry smile twisting his lips. "I'm sorry I didn't ask about protection."

My confusion must show because he lets out a dry laugh. "I know we were caught up in the heat of the moment, but I should have asked about not using a condom."

Oh. Oh!

"Honestly, it didn't cross my mind, either." I hadn't even thought of it. My cheeks grow warm as I peek over at him. "There's nothing to be worried about, right?"

Eric looks mortified, his electric blue eyes sparkling in the sunlight as they widen. "No! And if there was, I would have told you and definitely would have used protection."

"Okay." I shrug. "It's fine then, really. No need to worry." I give him a peck on the lips before winding my arm around his waist and leaning my head on his shoulder.

The intimacy doesn't last long because walking through the woods on a twisty trail full of knotted tree roots isn't ideal while you're in an embrace. His arm slips from around my shoulders, sliding down to tangle our fingers together.

"I actually have something kind of embarrassing to admit," he says quietly, as if he's afraid the trees will overhear his secret.

"What is it?" We switch places as the dogs tangle their leashes again, and I make a mental note to get one of those double leashes where they can cross and not get caught up. Though, on second thought, I'm not sure if that will work with their vast size difference.

"I haven't been with anyone since just after Daphne." He winces.

"Why is that embarrassing?" It's surprising, for sure. Eric seems like a highly sexual person, and it certainly didn't feel like he's been out of the game for years.

"I don't know, I guess because it kind of makes me seem a little hung up on her. I just haven't found anyone I was interested in," he peeks at me, "until now."

As we near the summit, the trail turns into switchbacks, and the terrain transforms into a steeper, rockier landscape. "I haven't been with anyone since Jonathan," I admit, keeping my eyes trained on my feet and periodically looking ahead to ensure it doesn't get too difficult for Bagel.

"Not even when you were in Europe?" I can hear the dry humor in his tone.

"I could have," I answer truthfully. "But something always held me back. After… After everything that happened, I didn't want something meaningless."

Archer hops over the last ridge, tail wagging and tongue flopping out of his mouth as he turns to see Bagel struggling to get up the lip of a smooth rock. My heart flutters, and my body explodes with a dopamine hit, like whenever I watch animal videos on social media, as Archer jumps back down and nudges Bagel under his butt, helping him up before jumping to the top once more.

Eric's hands are warm as he grips me from behind, sliding his palms under my shirt and against my skin as he helps me. While the view is beautiful, I imagine it will be breathtaking once the maple leaves have grown back, their bare gray branches resembling spindly fingers reaching between the evergreens.

"Alright, boys. Come get your snacks," Eric croons at the dogs as he kneels to get their bowls and food from his pack.

A slight breeze carries the scent of earthy moss and the unmistakable damp fragrance of spring. It's chilly, and I set my pack down to pull my sherpa-lined jean jacket over my flannel.

While Eric settles the dogs, I unwrap a granola bar and peer at the landscape. The forest stretches to the horizon, green speckled with gray and the occasional glimpse of a turquoise lake nestled amongst smaller peaks.

"This will be great for your travel blog," Eric murmurs, wrapping his arms around me. He's holding his phone horizontally, the camera flipped so the frame is filled with us and the dogs in the background.

Smiling while he takes a few shots, I reach an arm behind me to wind around his neck and press up on my tiptoes, balancing against his chest as I kiss him over my shoulder. Eric obliges me, snapping a few photos of us kissing before pulling back.

"So you're a fan of the blog, huh?" I ask, sitting on a large rock protruding from the ground.

His answer is merely a grin as he searches my pack for another granola bar.

Eventually, I'm startled when he asks, "Are you thinking about him?"

My gaze snaps to his, only to realize he's looking at my necklace. It takes me a second to realize I've fished it out from underneath my shirt and am rubbing the pads of my fingers over the alexandrite in the middle of the star.

"No!" I exclaim with so much zeal that it makes me sound guilty of doing exactly that. "I'm sorry, it's just a habit."

"It's okay, Evie. You don't have to hide it from me," he says softly, coming over and pressing a kiss against the top of my head. "I guess I'm just curious if I'll be spending my whole life sharing you with him."

Panic settles through my bones as viciously as the butterflies that erupt in my stomach at hearing him say he wants me for his whole life. I snap my head up to look at him. "No, Eric. I promise. It's not like that."

Except, it sort of is because as much as I try to forget about him, Jonathan *does* creep into my thoughts more often than I'd like. It makes me want to explain how I feel to Eric.

Don't let your past ruin your future.

I grab his hand and pull him down to sit beside me. He secures the dogs next to the rock before putting his arm around my shoulders and pulling me tightly against him.

"What I went through, spending those days there only to have Jonathan vanish into thin air like he never existed…it was *traumatic*. Even after we ran into each other—don't get me wrong, how could I be upset when his wife and daughter were alive? Still… it was also traumatic in its own way. Yet, therapeutic in a sense? I don't know if I'm making any sense–"

"You are," he interrupts. "I felt the same way with Daphne. Eight years is a long time to be with someone, especially when they spend most of it grieving. I wouldn't go as far as saying our divorce was traumatic, but it was hard to see her move on so quickly. Yet, at the same time, when I first saw them together, I understood right away, and I was happy for her."

"Understood what?"

"That she and Henry were meant to be together. Their story was like two pages of the same book that connected instantly as soon as they found each other."

I reflect on my ex-husband and how quickly he ruined our marriage for his secretary. "I'm sure that *was* hard to watch."

"Yeah, but I knew I'd find my own happy ending someday." He props his chin on my head and squeezes me tighter. "What I'm trying to say is, I understand if he sneaks into your thoughts occasionally. Daphne did, too, for over a year. It doesn't threaten me. I'll never get jealous of him or upset that he crosses your mind, and I'll never ask or expect you to stop wearing your necklace. It's a part of who you are now. I can't imagine you without that thing."

Again, the fact that we've only seen each other a handful of times since we met slinks into my head. Eric keeps making comments that suggest we've known each other for much longer.

"Besides, it's okay. I know I rock your world better than anyone can." I can hear the mirth in his tone, and I grin up at him to see a teasing smile on his face.

"You, sir, are one cocky man."

"Who, me?" He feigns shock and waves me off. "Nah. Maybe a little presumptuous, but not cocky," he exclaims with a, *'I would never,'* attitude.

"Presumptuous? Yeah, maybe just a little," I tease.

His demeanor turns serious. "I've known I want

you for a long time, Evie. I just manifested I'd get the chance, and when I did, I knew I needed to do whatever it took to keep you."

"Six weeks is a long time?"

His signature smirk sets my insides on fire, and for a moment, I wonder what it would be like to have sex on top of a mountain.

As though he knows precisely where my dirty thoughts have strayed, Eric maneuvers me back against the rock, covering my mouth with his in a heated kiss.

Archer whines, which causes Bagel to start making a commotion as well, and we laugh as we look at our poor pups, who are staring at us like they know we were about to scar them for life.

"Let's head back," Eric whispers against my lips before kissing me again. "I have a big dinner planned and then a *very* special dessert."

"I love dessert." I draw him down for another kiss. "Is it a surprise, or can I know what it is?"

"It's not a surprise." He shakes his head before smoothly transitioning into nodding it. "*Intimate* s'mores."

"Intimate?" I can only imagine what that means, and the anticipation of mixing chocolate and marshmallows with sex curls down my limbs, hot and heavy. "How do the graham crackers fit into that?" I ask with a lilt, arching my brow.

That damn sexy smirk crawls across his face again. "Baby, there are no graham crackers on this camping trip."

eric

"I told you, I got curious. I know what the ladies are into right now. Masked men, stalkers, being tied up and forced to have a million orgasms."

Evelyn's breath hitches as I nip her collarbone, and she cries out, "In books!" Her body undulates beneath mine, every soft inch of her melting against me as we make out on a blanket next to the fire.

Talking her into letting me have my dirty way with her is easy. My little tease is winding up by asking all these questions—her form of foreplay as she delays the inevitable.

Experiencing the darker side of me.

Truth be told, compared to what I've seen and read about, it's not even *that* dark. All I did was note which books she rated highly on her blog, then read them while taking notes and learning things about her that I'm not sure she even knows herself.

You can tell a lot about a person by their kinks.

"But what if I can make reality so much better than a fictional character on a page who can't touch you?" Snaking my hand beneath her shirt, I pull the cup of her bra down and palm a breast, rolling her nipple between my thumb and index finger. "Can't kiss you." Her skin is salty as I trace a path up her neck with my tongue. I suck on the spot below her ear and bury my face in her hair, inhaling the warm vanilla scent as it mixes with the unmistakable smell of campfire. "Can't fill you or fuck you the way you so desperately want." I roll my hips against hers, my cock straining so hard against my jeans that I'm careful not to give it too much friction, or I'll come in my fucking pants like a teenager. "I promise you'll be safe and satisfied and completely in control. The second you tell me to stop, I will."

"All this buildup for a boring safe word?" She pushes me back lightly, cupping the side of my neck while tangling her fingers in my hair—one delicate brow arched in amusement.

I can feel the rumble in my chest as it presses against hers. "Pick your word then, Evelyn."

One finger presses against her lips as she thinks about it before smiling and making an *aha* motion. "Gumdrop?"

I pause, staring at her for a hot second before an amused grin takes over my face. "Gumdrop? I feel like there's a story there."

Twisting her nipple, I relish the sharp gasp that flies from her throat before bending to take her in my mouth. My teeth clamp around the sensitive peak, tongue flicking against the bud.

"It's the first thing that came to my mind." Her voice is raspy and filled with anticipation as she holds my head to her chest. She likes having her nipples played with—licked, sucked, twisted, and pulled. I've never been with a woman so responsive when it comes to her breasts, but I know that when I pay hers extra attention, it makes her even wetter with want.

"You *do* love your food. I wouldn't expect anything less," I hum against her, looking up to see her eyes squeeze shut as she turns her head. It's her tell when she might be thinking about the man who gave her the necklace nestled in the hollow of her collarbone.

Tenderly, I grasp her chin and urge her to look back at me. "Stay with me, baby," I command gently.

Evelyn opens her beautiful blue eyes and stares up at me adoringly. "I'm with you. I promise."

"Do you trust me?" I ask, shifting back to sit on my knees.

"You know I do," she says before letting out a disappointed whimper when I rise to my feet and go to the fire to move the skillet I used to prepare our steaks for dinner earlier, swapping it for a small pot.

She sits up and watches curiously as I pour in some milk and break up a few chocolate bars, throwing them in and moving the pot to the far end of the cooktop so it doesn't melt too fast, or bubble over and burn.

"Is that for the s'mores?" I can hear the need heavy in her tone. The quiet rasp does nothing to hide how aroused she is, and it spurs my desire to have her at my complete mercy.

I don't reply as I zip the dogs into their tent, neither happy about being put away so early in the evening, but the sky is already dark, the stars shining brightly against the pitch-black canvas.

"Take off your clothes." I turn back to check on the melted chocolate mixture, noting the shock on her face. "Do it, Evelyn."

"Wh…what?" she stammers. Even though she looks surprised, her cheeks flush a pretty pink, and her eyes turn glassy with lust.

"You heard me, baby." Her eyes widen as I approach her and help her to her feet. "Remove all your clothes."

I don't have to tell her a third time. Evelyn starts to remove each piece slowly as I walk backward toward my truck, not wanting to miss a second of it. The air is warm from our fire, and a perfectly placed pine is at the edge of the site, so she won't get cold.

"What are you going to do with that?" she asks quietly as I pull a bundle of rope from the floor of the backseat. She wraps her arms around her middle, clad in only her bra and underwear.

"Don't hide from me, Evelyn. I want to see all of you." I return to her and tip her chin up, consuming her lips as I reach around to undo her bra clasps. She lets me finish undressing her, swallowing a thick gulp as I slowly lower her panties until I'm face level with her most intimate parts.

Leaning forward, I press a kiss just above her clit. Her whimper is like music to my ears, and she doesn't question when I urge her backward with further kisses, always just narrowly missing the spot where she wants my mouth the most.

"What are you doing?" she asks as I tie each of her legs to a post in the ground. I put them here earlier when she was taking photos of the lake, knowing that this is where tonight would end up because I know deep down she wants to have an experience she's only read about.

"Shh, you said you trust me." I lick up her center as I rise, shoving my tongue in her mouth while I gather her wrists above her head. In no time at all, she's secured to the rope I swung over a lower branch earlier, stretched out naked and entirely at my mercy.

Evie

"God, you're so fucking beautiful," Eric whispers as he takes me in.

"And I thought you were a nice guy? Nice guys don't tie women to trees." I'm amused and, if I'm being honest, more than a little turned on. It's thrilling, and I trust him one hundred percent to not do anything that will hurt me.

Plus, he's completely right about being better

than a fictional character. This is something I thought I'd only enjoy in my smutty romance novels, but this is looking promising and he hasn't even started with the dessert.

"I try hard to be a nice guy, Evelyn. But one thing I've come to learn about women is that they don't *want* a nice guy." He pulls the knot tight, the fabric digging into my wrists as he finishes securing them. My chest rises and falls in rapid succession and my eyes snap to where he pulls a strip of black cloth from his pocket. "Well, they *do* want a nice guy. But we have to be able to read your minds, don't we? We have to know when you want the gentleman and when you want the fantasy. When it's time to pull your chair out for you and when it's time to bend you over that chair and fuck you until you pass out."

Warmth blossoms in my lower belly, despite the chill in the air, as he places the fabric behind my head and brings both sides around to cover my mouth. I squirm against the tree even though the bark is rough against my back, trying to create any sort of friction to ease the pressure in my aching pussy.

"Even though no one is supposed to be around, I have a feeling you're gonna get loud, and I don't want to share those sounds with anyone." Eric chuckles darkly, the shadows from the campfire dancing across his face like some sort of henchmen praising their evil villain.

Only, I want this villain to win. I want him to do depraved things to me. Then I want him to make me a damn s'more and feed me before doing it all over again.

"So, welcome to the fantasy you didn't know you wanted," he whispers against my lips.

Turning away, he goes back to the fire, stirring the chocolate before grabbing a skewer he made from a branch earlier and the bag of marshmallows sitting on the picnic table.

He pulls his chair over, sitting down and resting his elbows on his forearms as he puts one of the puffy white globs on the sharpened end and holds it over the fire.

Uh, hello, buddy? I'm strung up naked and gagged over here, and you're not gonna get undressed and ravish me?

"Patience, baby," he says in response to the question I definitely didn't ask out loud. "Perfection takes time." He doesn't look at me as he roasts the mallow, rotating the skewer slowly in a continuous motion. "You know the secret to a perfectly roasted marshmallow?"

Finally he looks at me, that wicked grin of his spearing his lips wide enough to show me his perfect teeth. When I shake my head, he looks back to the fire. "It's patience. You see, you want the inside to be all melted and the outside to have that perfect golden brown crisp to it."

Hooking his ankle around a leg of the chair, he spins it in my direction, suddenly looking like the devil incarnate. He reaches for the skin of the mallow, pulling it off to reveal the melted white treasure below. Popping the skin in his mouth, he holds the skewer in my direction. For a moment, I think he's going to try and feed me even though I'm gagged, however, it takes me a second to register that he's spreading the warm sticky goo all over my breast.

An immediate flood of arousal escapes my pussy, coating the insides of my thighs as I let out a loud, rough moan. It's only uncomfortable for a second before the pain gives way to pleasure.

"That's my girl. You love being covered in sweets, don't you, baby? Because you know I'm going to lick it all up and clean it off you later," Eric croons as he returns what's left of the mallow to the fire.

My breaths are labored as he removes the skin a second time, dipping the marshmallow in the melted chocolate before returning it to my body. He covers the other nipple and I squeal around the gag, the temperature more scalding than the first pass, as he turns me into his own Charleston Chew.

"Is it too hot?" he asks, sounding only mildly concerned and more amused than anything.

Shaking my head as my pussy clenches around air, I arch my back the best I can in my bound position, begging for his mouth.

It's not until he's painted down my stomach and over my thighs that he finally stands and scoops the melted dessert from the skewer before approaching me. He lifts his fingers between us, blowing on the warm mixture of goo. "I'm going to thoroughly enjoy eating *my* dessert from between your legs."

It's warm, not hot, as he spreads it over my clit. Tears line my eyes, not from the pain, but from the pure frustration at being at his mercy yet not having him touch me until just now. It's ecstasy, the way his fingers strum my swollen bud and then dip between my wet folds.

I'm definitely getting a UTI...but it's so fucking worth it.

Eric sucks the mess from his fingers before removing his clothes, revealing his sculpted body and the gorgeous cock that points directly at me. He lowers to his knees, kissing down my body and around the trail of mess he's made, before he gets to my pussy.

Scooping my legs into the crook of his elbows, I realize there's more give to the rope that binds my ankles as he effortlessly lifts me before attacking my clit. His warm tongue swirls and strokes as he moans against me, and the sensations of the bark at my back and his mouth between my thighs clash against each other like warriors on a battlefield.

Pain versus pleasure.

I come hard with a scream that echoes through the woods, despite the gag. White spots blind my vision until I become boneless in his arms, sagging against the ropes that hold me up as he swallows me down before licking up the trail of sweets he's decorated my body with.

"So fucking perfect," he whispers against me, lowering my feet to the ground.

Without looking at me, he pulls the gag from my

mouth at the same time he latches onto a nipple. I don't know what it is about this man and my nipples, but every time he has them in his mouth, he knows how to manipulate them in a way that makes it feel like he's still sucking on my clit.

"Eric," I whine. "I need you inside me."

"Does my good girl want to get fucked against the tree?" he asks before turning his attention to my other breast. He nearly has me clean and I can feel his solid, warm erection between us, just waiting for its turn.

Looking down at it, I lick my lips. "Unless you want to untie me so I can have my dessert, too?"

Eric moans. It's not a groan, but a sensual sound that I want to hear again and again like a personal lullaby as he fucks me to sleep. "Baby, I need to fuck you. We have all night for you to eat your dessert off my dick."

There's no warning as he presses inside me, my walls stretching to accommodate him in a vice-like grip that has us both drawing sharp-pitched breaths. I strain against the ropes holding my arms up, a pins and needles sensation starting to settle in my limbs from how long they've been in this position.

There's nothing slow or sweet about the way Eric takes his pleasure. His thrusts are long and deep and his fingers dig into my skin as he takes me hard against the tree.

"God, I love the way you feel. Your pussy sucks my cock in like it never wants me to leave."

"Because you give it everything it wants without

even having to ask," I speak into his mouth as his lips rest over mine. We don't kiss, but the intimacy of simply being this close is more sensual than a kiss would be at this moment.

"Thanks to those romance books you're always reading." He releases a short, shuddered laugh as he picks up his pace, thrusting into me at a punishing rate.

Awareness prickles down my spine, but I can't tell if it's another impending orgasm or something else. "How do you know what books I read?"

It's an odd time to ask such a question, but he's been saying things like this all weekend. And earlier, on the mountain, when I asked if he was a fan of my blog…

"So you stalked me?" I grin as I make the poorly timed joke.

More men should be open to learning from romance novels.

"I've been stalking you for an entire year, Evelyn."

His thrusts become erratic as the weight of his admission spreads through my chest.

"*What*?"

Eric slows, his breathing heavy as he drops his lips to my neck and alternates between licking and sucking the skin. My walls clench around him as he pulls nearly all the way out before slowly inching his way back in, his tip just barely brushing that sweet spot with every pass.

"The girls told me about you last year," he whispers. "Naturally, I was curious." He bends to suck one nipple into his mouth, manipulating it with his teeth and tongue and expertly causing my clit to pulse. "I've been watching you for a long time—longer than New Years."

I wonder if I should feel some sense of betrayal at his news, but all I can focus on is the way his hips keep angling so that the tip of his cock drives into me deeper and deeper. "Fuck, I've dreamed about this pussy swallowing my cock." *Thrust.* He pops off my chest to watch where he keeps disappearing inside me. "I studied every single post you made." *Thrust.* "Read every book you rated highly." *Thrust.* "And examined you for months after I realized you're literally my dream girl."

I want to cry from the onslaught of emotions pouring through me. I've never felt pleasure like this while at the same time experiencing panic.

Is he seriously a real stalker?

Does it fucking matter with how good he's fucking you? He's obsessed with you. He figured out all the things you like just so he could bring you pleasure. So what if he stalked you for a few months?

Eric chuckles. "You might be thinking I sound insane, but, baby, I'm just fucking *obsessed*." He groans against my lips as he devours them again. He tastes like chocolate and marshmallow and *me*.

Kissing him back passionately, I grip the rope tighter, and my toes curl while I attempt to take him in as far as he'll go. Eric releases a long moan, which heightens my arousal, pressing me harder against the scratchy bark of the tree.

Suddenly, it hits me that his confession doesn't even phase me. It doesn't scare me or make me think he's a creep because he's done nothing except take the time to learn about me so that he can understand me—what makes me who I am and what he can do to appeal to my likes and interests, even though it's clear I would have liked him without any of that.

"Let me go," I plead against his lips. "Undo the ropes, Eric."

"I'll do it because you asked so nicely." He nips my bottom lip. "But I'm never letting you go, Evelyn."

I'm more than okay with that.

He remains inside me as he quickly releases my wrists, somehow not slipping from between my legs even as he pulls us down once I'm free. Eric sinks to the ground with me straddling him, and his head falls back as I take over the pace, riding him with sharp jerks of my hips. Each thrust makes my breasts bounce as he taps my G-Spot.

"Fuck, baby. You ride me so well. Such a greedy little slut for my cock, aren't you?" he moans.

I'll never get tired of hearing the sounds he makes while I bring him pleasure. I never thought a man moaning would be such a huge turn-on. "I am. I fucking love your cock."

I also love that you researched ways to bring me pleasure. I love that you adore me and want to make me happy. I love…

"I love *you,*" he says, moving his hands to my hips as he pounds into me from underneath. "I fucking love you, Evelyn."

My release rips through me, and I tip my head back and watch the stars as I ride out my orgasm. A flood of warmth pours between us, like some ethereal experience as we come together. Wave after wave crests through me. I drop forward, connecting our lips as I continue to milk him until we're a mess of shaking limbs and pitchy moans that escape our mouths on sated sighs.

"I love you, too," I whisper against his lips. "As for studying me, we'll have to talk about that. I feel like that's cheating." I laugh playfully, not an ounce of terror or displeasure in my bones.

"I know. And I'm sorry. I was just so sure you were made for me after reading only a few of your posts. Not just physically, but emotionally, as well. I'm sorry I didn't tell you sooner. I just didn't want you to think I was creepy." He looks so sincere as he wipes my sweaty hair off my face.

"Creepier than bringing me to the woods to tie me up and eat melted marshmallows and chocolate off me?" I tease, stretching to peck his lips. "Seriously, though. I think it's the nicest thing anyone has ever done for me."

"Tied you up and turned you into a giant graham cracker? Damn, the bar is low." He laughs, reaching for the corner of the blanket to pull it around us.

We cuddle in our post-coital bliss as we watch the

twinkling stars above. "I don't want to go back tomorrow," he confesses.

I don't reply because the thought of returning to the city has me thinking of how he'll have to start traveling for work again. So, I remain quiet, eventually falling asleep in Eric's arms beneath the starry night sky.

evie

Eric untangles our fingers for the sixth time in the last ten minutes. Expelling a frustrated growl, he reaches for his phone, which is attached to a holder on his dash.

"What?" he gruffly answers.

Over the sound of the road and Archer and Bagel playing in the backseat, I can barely make out someone frantically yelling on the other end of the line. Shifting toward the window, I try not to let my own frustrated sigh loose.

The trees have turned back into buildings, the outer city limits racing by as we head back.

"Look, I told you before I left that you would have to take care of it. You want that CISO title someday? You're going to have to earn it. I shouldn't have to hold your hand at this point in your career. You know what you're doing. You got this. Now, stop calling me, and let me finish my vacation in peace."

He hangs up the phone and slides it back into the

holder, but when he reaches for my hand again, I keep it curled in my lap.

"Sorry about that," he apologizes.

"Don't worry about it," I offer quietly, leaning my head against the cool glass.

"Are you okay?" he sounds worried. It's a far cry from how we've spent the last twenty-four hours, but now that we've returned to the real world, all the problems we still have to face are racing toward us at the speed of light.

"If I'm being honest, I'm a little worried now that we're back." I shift back toward him, picking at my nails as I avoid his eyes.

"What are you worried about, baby?" He covers my hands with his, allowing no room to object as he intertwines our fingers again.

Taking a deep breath, I decide to voice my concerns instead of sitting on them. Besides, I already told Eric once I didn't want to come second to a job again. "Your job is demanding. You're always gone, and while I love to travel, don't get me wrong, I just can't imagine going back and forth to New York that much. When are we ever going to have time to see each other?"

He pulls my hand over to kiss my knuckles. "You don't have to worry about that, Evelyn. I won't be traveling any longer."

Surprise hits me like a freight train. "What do you mean?"

That damn sexy grin spreads across his face as he leans an elbow on the center console and kisses my hand again. "I told my company I needed to scale back—no more travel, unless we're on vacation. I need to be stationary here in Chicago and can't be on call like I have been."

"Eric, you love your job. Please tell me you didn't do that for me. The last thing I need is for you to wake up one day and resent me."

"Baby, stop. I told them I found the woman I plan on starting a family with, whether that means us and the dogs, or kids, if you decide you want to adopt. That means more to me than any job," he explains.

Tears prick my eyes, my sinuses burning as I try to hold them at bay. I'm overcome with gratitude, and then I remember he asked for time off before he returned for that dinner where we ran into each other at the restaurant. "You told them that? But you put in for time off before you even came back to Chicago."

Eric releases a booming laugh that fills the cab as he pulls into my parking lot. "Honestly, I told my boss I'd met my future wife as soon as I returned to the table the night we sexted."

A laugh bubbles up in my throat, and as soon as the truck is parked, I undo my seatbelt and launch myself across the truck to embrace him. "I love you. Thank you."

"I love you, too. There's no need to thank me."

"No, seriously, Eric. You're incredible, and I'm so lucky you love me." My tears flow freely, prompting Bagel to whine from the backseat because my pup is always in tune with my emotions. His cries cause Archer to start chiming in, and Eric and I laugh as our hounds start their tune of sympathy.

"Knock that off, you rascals." He turns and scratches Archer's head before scooping Bagel from the back and pulling him into his lap. "What do you think, kiddo? You want to keep living here with your fancy elevators and no yard? Or do you wanna come out to the burbs and stretch your legs?"

Bagel gives him a "Whoo! Whoo!" before jumping up to lick his face.

"You want us to move in with you?" I have to admit, even though we've already said *I love you,* I wasn't expecting him to want us to move in so quickly.

"I told you, Evelyn, there doesn't need to be a time limit on it. If you'd rather stay in your own place, I respect that. But, eventually, it just makes sense for you to move in. Doesn't it? There's lots of space, a huge yard, and enough rooms for you to set up an office if you want."

"You've really thought this through, haven't you?" My heart skips a beat, warming with his intentions.

I don't know how I managed to get so lucky. Even if he did stalk me. Even if he's *obsessed* with me. Doesn't every woman want that? Doesn't every woman *deserve* that?

"I told you, I've been waiting for you for a long time, Evelyn. I'm all in. I don't need time to decide that." He reaches over and cups my cheek in his palm.

I tilt my head into it. "Promise me this is real? That I won't wake up tomorrow to find it was all a dream."

Eric places Bagel next to Archer and pushes his seat back before pulling me into his lap. "I promise you, Evelyn soon-to-be Adams, that while I will spend the rest of our lives making your world as dreamlike as possible, it will all be real."

"You are my dream, though." I lean my forehead against his. "You crashed into my world like a supernova. Just promise me your love won't fade."

He kisses the tip of my nose before pressing his lips against mine in a short but firm kiss. "I promise, baby. I will love you until the stars abandon the sky in search of other galaxies, and even then, I'll find a way for us to follow them."

I release a shuddered laugh and pull back to wipe my tears. "Okay, you have to stop reading the romance novels."

"Never." He leans forward, kissing the hollow of my throat where my North Star pendant rests. "Besides, Archer is partial to the smutty audiobooks."

"Oh, yeah?" I peer behind the seat at the giant German shepherd, who cocks his head at me. "Well, we can't stop listening to *those*, now can we?"

"Whoo! Whoo! Whoo!"

epilogue

Evie

Three Years Later

"Everyone, we'd like to introduce you to Nova Marie Adams." I prop my toddler on my hip, turning so everyone can see her.

Nova stares at them all with carefully guarded eyes the color of a tiger's eye stone. At only three years old, the little girl has been through hell and back, losing her parents to a house fire only to have her relatives refuse to take her in.

Their loss is Eric's and my gain. As soon as we met her, we knew she was our daughter. Our little supernova.

Nova turns and looks at me before sliding her eyes to Eric and reaching for him wordlessly. She's a quiet and timid little girl, so we waited a few weeks to introduce her to our friends.

Eric pulls her into his arms, and she buries her face in the crook of his neck as Daphne walks over slowly.

"Hi there, Nova. It's so nice to meet you. I have a

daughter your age. Would you like to meet her?" Daphne coos softly.

Slowly, Nova nods, and Eric and I share a tearful glance.

Before Daphne can call for her daughter—who is sitting on Bree's son, Liam's, lap at the table, coloring—Rose jumps down with a gleeful, high-pitched squeal. "Santa is real, Mommy! Daddy, look! Santa brought me a late Christmas present!"

"A late Christmas present? What did you ask Santa for, sweetheart?" Henry asks her, casting a confused look in Daphne's direction because I'm sure they got everything Rose requested on her list.

The little blonde skips over, her pigtails bouncing with each leap as she cries, "I asked for a sibling! Now I have a sister!"

Liam sarcastically calls out behind her, "Well, geez, little thorn. What? Am I not good enough for you?"

Eric kneels as Nova shyly picks her head up to examine Rose. I'm not even aware tears are streaming from my eyes until Daphne puts a hand on my back, rubbing it soothingly.

"Hi! I'm Rose!"

Nova looks up at me, then at Eric, before settling back on Rose. "I'm Nova."

Rose launches herself at our daughter, pulling her into a tight hug. "We're going to be best friends! Come color with me!"

Nova scrunches her little face as Rose pulls her toward the kitchen table.

Eric stands and wraps his arm around my waist, leaning in to kiss my temple. "If anyone can help her come out of her shell, it'll be Roselyn."

Henry comes to stand next to Daphne, mirroring our position as we all watch our daughters together. "They're gonna be trouble when they get older."

"Oh, trust me. They're going to be trouble *now*," Bree exclaims as she joins us. "You know I lost Rose for an hour the other day? She was hiding beneath Liam's bed and refused to come out until he got home."

I can't help but laugh. Little Rose is obsessed with Bree's son, and none of us can see her obsession letting up anytime soon. "Maybe she'll direct her focus to Nova now."

"She's adorable," Daphne says, looking at us with a sparkle in her eyes. "I'm so happy for you both."

"We sure got lucky," I sigh, watching Bree's other kids say hello to their new pseudo-cousin. With every passing second, Nova seems to brighten, more sure of herself than I've seen her since we brought her home. "Look at her. She's thriving. Maybe we should have introduced them sooner. Are we already bad parents?"

Eric turns me so I'm facing him. "Baby, relax. We're not bad parents. Too much *new* wasn't the way to acclimate her."

"I know, I know, I just–"

"Evelyn, stop," he gently commands. "You're a great mother. Stop worrying." He spins me around and wraps his arms around my middle, resting his chin on my shoulder. "She's perfect, isn't she?"

I watch Nova smile as Rose shares her coloring book. Her warm, golden brown eyes lift to meet mine, her smile widening as she waves at us.

There was a time when I never could have even dreamed this would be possible—that I'd be a wife again and a mother to an incredible little girl. My husband has made all my dreams come true, and brings new ones to life every single day.

And I couldn't be happier.

"Yes." I lean my head against his. "She really is."

Eric

"Are my girls ready for dessert?"

Archer yips playfully, jumping up to try and get to my platter of sweets as I cross the backyard.

By the roaring fire pit, Evie and Nova gaze at the stars while wrapped in a blanket. My daughter sits on my wife's lap while Bagel lies in hers.

There's been a significant change in Nova in the weeks since we introduced her to Rose. She's come out of her shell more, expressing more interest in us and the dogs than when we first brought her home.

It broke our hearts to see her file, and we knew she was *our* little girl right away—the one we'd been waiting for.

"Daddy, did you get the fluff?" Nova asks.

Evie and I look at each other wide-eyed because she's never called me Dad before.

I sniff back the tears that prick my eyes, trying not to let the emotion overcome me so I don't scare her. "Sure did, honey, and the peanut butter cups you love so much."

Sitting beside them on the giant swing that usually resides on our porch, I set the platter on a small table, directing Archer to lie by my feet and giving him an elk antler so our energetic pup doesn't keep trying to get into our food.

"Mommy?" Nova turns to look up at Evie, and I can see my wife struggling to keep her tears in.

"Yes, baby?" she responds shakily.

"I love you guys. I'm glad you're my mommy and daddy now."

I place my arm around Evie's shoulders, pulling them into my side as I drop a kiss on the top of Nova's head. "We love you, too, baby girl."

Words can't describe the influx of emotions running through me. My chest swells with so much love and gratitude that it nearly feels like I'm having a heart attack.

Can you die from loving so hard?

If so, I'll happily perish as long as my girls are taken care of.

Knowing my wife, though, she'll find a way to bring me back just to kill me again for leaving her.

I look at Evelyn, our gazes locking over Nova's head.

I love you, I mouth to her.

I love you, too, she mouths back.

Then, cuddled up with my girls beneath the starry night sky, I make my beautiful wife a s'more.

afterword

After I finished Peppermint Wishes, I honestly wasn't sure Evie and Eric would get their story. I was ready to start my next project, and neither of them was talking to me enough to keep writing—even though the readers wanted more from them.

Fast forward to early winter. I had nothing new to share with my readers. The project I'd been working on for months was unavailable to talk about, and I realized I had nothing to release. I'll forever be grateful to my friend and best biscuit, A.R. Rose, who listened to every frantic voice message and helped me realize that now was the perfect time to finish Evie and Eric's story, even though it had been a year since Peppermint Wishes released.

I wrote this book in three weeks. I had nothing for it when I started, but it didn't take long for Eric to convince me he had everything covered, and all I had to do was write what he told me. I think he'd been itching to get his story since Where the Flowers

Bloom ended, but I'm a big believer in everything happening for a reason, and though it took a while, I can say with absolute certainty that I am obsessed with this story.

From how Eric was so sure about Evie from the moment he heard about her to how Evie wasn't afraid when she learned he'd been watching her for quite some time, their story was just beautiful.

It was a missing piece I didn't know the Darby-verse needed in order to move on to the next generation.

And now every time I look up at the starry night sky, I'll never forget this magical weekend in the woods.

acknowledgments

I don't think there will ever be another book I write where I don't want to give a million thank you's to my team. Alex, Jessica, Cady, Ashley, Lauren, and April, I am fully convinced that my stories wouldn't be as great without you ladies. Thank you for loving my characters as much as I do.

Virginia Carey, my editor, thank you so much for squeezing me in before your vacation. I know I really pushed the limits by setting such a short release date, so I thank you for taking the time to fit me into your schedule.

WallFlower Designs, I'm so obsessed with these covers. You really brought my imagination to life on such short notice and I'll be forever grateful!

And to the readers who wanted more, who wanted Evie to get her true happily ever after without discounting her Christmas at Sutton Lake, thank you so much for encouraging me to give her and Eric the happy ending they deserved.

about the author

D.L. Darby lives in Anchorage, Alaska. She's a fur momma to her dog and cat and a superwife to her husband.

By day, she's a hairstylist, and by night, she's continuously drafting new ideas on her murder board at home. When she's not working, reading, or writing, you can find her glued to the TV, bingeing whatever new reality show Netflix has created.

Made in the USA
Middletown, DE
06 February 2025

70261390R00092